"I think I

Anna gently pressed her tea bag with a spoon before removing it from the cup. "For crying like that before. I'm not... I don't usually behave that way."

Jeremiah shook his head. "You owe me nothing. I'm sorry I woke you, bringing the dog into the house and making such a racket. No wonder you were upset."

"It wasn't that. It's just..." She managed a half laugh. "I thought you were someone else."

"Vass?" The word choked out of Jeremiah's throat.

"Only for a second." She hurried to explain. "I was dreaming. I guess I heard you come in the kitchen like Henry used to, and somehow—"

"You don't have to explain." Jeremiah sounded determined. "Today was a hard day. You were overtired."

"That's so," Anna agreed, dropping her gaze to her tea mug. She'd embarrassed him, talking so free. She'd not meant to.

"Anna?"

She looked up. *"Ja?"*

"Don't fret yourself. It's all right." His expression was a mixture of sympathy and support. "You're going to be all right."

Laurel Blount lives on a small farm in Georgia with her husband, David, their four children, a milk cow, dairy goats, assorted chickens, an enormous dog, three spoiled cats and one extremely bossy goose with boundary issues. She divides her time between farm chores, homeschooling and writing, and she's happiest with a cup of steaming tea at her elbow and a good book in her hand.

Books by Laurel Blount

Love Inspired

A Family for the Farmer
A Baby for the Minister
Hometown Hope
A Rancher to Trust
Lost and Found Faith
Her Mountain Refuge
Together for the Twins
A Family to Foster
The Triplets' Summer Adventure

Hickory Springs Amish

The Amish Widower's Surprise
Trusting the Amish Farmer

Visit the Author Profile page at LoveInspired.com.

TRUSTING THE AMISH FARMER

LAUREL BLOUNT

LOVE INSPIRED
INSPIRATIONAL ROMANCE

ISBN-13: 978-1-335-62102-3

Trusting the Amish Farmer

Copyright © 2025 by Laurel Blount

Recycling programs for this product may not exist in your area.

Love Inspired
22 Adelaide St. West, 41st Floor
Toronto, Ontario M5H 4E3, Canada
www.LoveInspired.com

Printed in Lithuania

MIX
Paper | Supporting responsible forestry
FSC® C021394

For God hath not given us the spirit of fear;
but of power, and of love, and of a sound mind.
—*2 Timothy* 1:7

For my husband, David, with all my love

Chapter One

Anna Speicher was clenching the reins so tightly that her knuckles had gone white. The closer the buggy got to the old Speicher farm, the harder her heart pounded.

She was being silly, she told herself. If she wanted to sell her late husband's farm, she had to meet the buyer there so he could walk the place over.

And, of course, she did want to sell—for a very good reason.

Anna glanced down at her two-year-old son, sitting beside her on the buggy seat. Matthew was staring sleepily over the mare's back, his short legs dangling well above the floorboard. As if feeling his *mamm*'s gaze, he looked up and smiled.

As she smiled back, Anna's pounding heart slowed, and her determination strengthened.

Ja. She was selling the farm. And the sooner, the better.

She'd thought this through carefully. Her husband's older siblings didn't agree, but none of them wanted to buy the farm, and the place had been sitting empty for nearly three years. Besides, now that Henry was gone, this was her decision to make.

So, she'd made it. After six generations, the old farm was passing out of the Speicher family.

When she'd come to it as a bride, the Speicher farm had seemed so perfect—a hundred acres of green rolling hills with spacious barns and a white farmhouse the ideal size for raising a big family. The land boasted the best soil and finest pastures in Hickory Springs, Tennessee, and she'd felt incredibly blessed that her husband, Henry, the youngest son, was the one given the property. His father had died years before, and after their wedding, Henry's mother planned to go live with one of her daughters two counties over, so they'd have the place to themselves—until the *kinder* started coming along. A few months later, when Anna had found out she was expecting, she'd been so happy. All her dreams were coming true.

Then the farm had broken her heart, like it had broken the hearts of so many other women in the Speicher family. As if the long days and backbreaking work hadn't been enough, three years ago, Henry had been killed in an accident at harvest time, just as his father had been years before—and a great-grandfather before that.

The farm wasn't done causing her problems, even then. Since Henry's death, Anna had been pestered relentlessly by profit-minded men who saw her and the farm as an attractive package deal. Marry the twenty-five-year-old widow, gain a valuable property in an area where land prices had gone through the roof. She'd received no fewer than eight proposals over the past two years, two of them written in letters by men she'd never so much as laid eyes on.

Enough was enough.

With the farm gone, she'd be left in peace with her decision to remain unmarried. Well, mostly. Her mother wouldn't be happy, for certain sure.

Neither would Henry's siblings. They wanted her to pass

the family property down to Matthew, born six months after his father's death, but she had no intention of doing so.

Her son would never be a farmer. Anna snapped the reins on her mare's back and sat up straighter on the buggy seat. *Nee*, Matthew would be a storekeeper, like her own *daed* had been. A nice respectable, *safe* storekeeper.

She was going to see to it. Starting today.

When they pulled into the driveway, Matthew's eyes widened. "Look, Mamm! Big wagon!" Like most little boys, he was fascinated by anything with wheels, and the bigger the better.

And the wagon parked by the barn was plenty big. A delivery wagon from the looks of it, so this must be the potential buyer her landlady, Susie Raber, had told her about.

"*Ja*, I see! That belongs to the man Mamm needs to talk to." Anna glanced down at the envelope in her lap, double-checking the name. "Jeremiah."

Jeremiah Weaver was from the neighboring Plain community over in Owl Hollow, but he worked for a company that made deliveries to the bakery where Susie worked. Anna had never met him, but for some reason she couldn't comprehend, he wanted to be a farmer.

Anna was secretly glad she didn't know the fellow. She'd not have wished a farmer's life on anybody, and it would be easier to sell the place to someone she wasn't well acquainted with. She felt a bit guilty even selling it to a stranger, although Susie had assured her she shouldn't.

"It's the best farm in the whole county," Susie had told her. "It hasn't been a happy place for you, I understand that." Susie was a widow herself, so likely she did. "But that doesn't mean it can't be a fine home for another family. And then you'll have the money to start up that specialty grocery store you keep talking about. There's no reason to feel guilty. Jeremiah's a grown man, and he can think for himself. He's a real strong fellow, too, and a hard worker. He can make a go of farming, if anybody can."

Anna had privately doubted anybody could nowadays, but she didn't argue. She did, however, have a question.

"Is this Jeremiah married?"

"*Nee*, he isn't." Susie had shot her a speculative glance, and Anna had flushed. She should have been more careful. Susie was well known for her matchmaking, and if she thought Anna had changed her mind about marrying again, she'd never be able to resist meddling. "He was supposed to be, but he and the girl broke things off two days before the wedding. Most of the cooking was already done." Susie clucked her tongue. *"Sis en shand."*

Ja, such behavior was a disgrace for sure, but the news had made Anna feel a bit better. So, Jeremiah Weaver was the sort of fellow who made a bride have second thoughts, was he? Maybe such a man deserved to be a farmer.

Anyway, Susie was right. Anna needed the money if she wanted to get her little grocery store up and running. She'd agreed to meet with Jeremiah this afternoon so he could look the place over and make his decision.

As she pulled the buggy to a stop, a man walked out of the main barn, just as if he already owned the place. Anna felt a flicker of irritation. Jeremiah Weaver had wasted no time making himself at home.

"Big man," Matthew whispered, his eyes round.

"Shh," Anna said. But Susie had told the truth—this Jeremiah did look strong. He was tall and broad-shouldered, with muscles that strained the sleeves of his blue shirt. His hair was dark brown and had an unruly look to it.

"Good afternoon," she called. She set the brake, tucked the envelope under arm and hopped down. "You'll be Jeremiah Weaver." She beckoned to Matthew, who obediently slid across the seat toward her. She swung him out of the buggy and set him on the ground beside her.

"Ja," the man agreed in a deep voice. "And you'll be Anna." He waited by the barn door while she and Matthew walked in his direction. "Who's this you've brought with you?"

"This is my son, Matthew."

"Nice to meet you, Matthew."

Her son stared up wordlessly, stunned into silence. And small wonder. The man looked even bigger close up. Henry had been no small fellow, but this Jeremiah would have towered over him. He must be well over six feet. Closer to seven.

The man's face gentled as he contemplated the awestruck child, but he didn't speak again, nor move a muscle. The way he held himself, so still, tickled a childhood memory. He reminded her of something…but what?

She didn't know, and it didn't matter, anyhow. Best get down to business.

"Susie Raber says you're looking for a farm?"

He moved his gaze from Matthew's face to hers. "I am, *ja.*"

She waited, but apparently Jeremiah was a man of few words. "I see you've already checked over the barn."

If he could tell she wasn't pleased about that, he gave no sign. "I have."

"And?"

"It'll suit. Needs some work, but nothing I can't manage." He studied her with thoughtful eyes, almost the same dark brown color as his hair. "Other things want fixing, too."

She frowned. "Like what?"

"Lots of scrub pines coming up in the fields, and a couple of trees down on the fence behind that little pond."

The pond. She and Henry had gone fishing there in the summer. She'd pack a picnic, and—

Anna shook her head, willing the memories away. "The pond's on the back edge of the property. You've already walked the whole place over?"

He shrugged. "I got here early, so I poked around, figuring it would save us some time. Seen pretty much everything except the house. You can show me over that, and then we'll talk terms."

Terms. Anna's heartbeat quickened, and she held out the envelope. "I've written all that down."

She'd thought that best—to write it all down. She didn't want any misunderstandings, and she knew once she was on the farm there'd be Matthew—and old memories—to deal with. She'd never had to conduct such an important business deal before, and she needed to get a good price on this place, a fair price.

Jeremiah made no move to take the envelope. "I thought we'd just talk it over." Another long pause. "I expected you'd bring some fellow along with you to settle the deal." His gaze dropped to Matthew, and one corner of his mouth tipped up. "An older fellow, I mean. Your *daed* or a brother, maybe."

He didn't want to talk business with a woman? Anna straightened her shoulders. Well, too bad. He was going to have to.

"My *daed* has passed away, and I don't have any brothers, only sisters. Besides, this farm belongs to me." She wiggled the envelope. "I wrote everything down," she repeated.

He sighed. "All right, then." He took the envelope from

her hand, slowly and gently. Memory stirred again, and this time she recognized it.

Daed's old Percheron, Amos. That's what Jeremiah reminded her of. The gentle horse had moved in just the same way, as if aware how his huge size could startle a person. She'd fed Amos apple slices as a child, and she remembered how carefully he'd taken the treats, his lips brushing her palm as lightly as a butterfly's wing.

"I guess you'd best show me the house," Jeremiah said, startling her out of her thoughts.

She blinked. "Of course."

Taking Matthew's hand, she led the way across the yard toward the front porch. "The furniture goes with the house. If you decide you want the place, there are some personal things that I'll have to get out, but that shouldn't take long."

Without turning to look, she knew Jeremiah had followed. The porch floor shook under his steps as she turned the key in the lock and pushed the door open.

"This is the living room." She picked Matthew up before stepping back to allow Jeremiah to walk inside.

She'd almost forgotten the scent of her old home. In fact, she'd never have thought it had a special smell, but, of course, it did. It was still here, a little musty, maybe, but heartbreakingly familiar. As she breathed it in, such a flood of memories struck her that she was glad Jeremiah was too busy looking around the room to pay any attention to her.

She and Henry had arranged the furniture here. Polished this wooden floor that was now filmed over with dust. She should have come here a day or two ago and swept it over— and beaten the rug clean, too.

She'd tied that rag rug together herself, begging for scraps in the right colors from her own sisters and her new sisters-in-law. She'd been so happy with how it had turned out, not too lumpy. She'd imagined her baby crawling across it one day, but, of course, that had never happened.

She glanced down at Matthew. He yawned and nestled his head against her collarbone, clearly bored. This house that had meant so much to her and Henry meant nothing to him.

Which was good, all things considered. But somehow, sad, too.

"Anna?" Jeremiah's voice made her jump. He was looking at her, his forehead creased. "Are you all right?"

"I—" She swallowed. "I'm fine." Her voice sounded strange, too high and shaky.

He regarded her silently for a second. When he spoke, his voice was quiet—and gentle.

"I'm very sorry," he said. "Susie told me you'd lost your husband."

"*Ja*, but not…not recently," she explained, embarrassed. "It's been three years now."

"Still."

Just one word, but somehow it touched the sorest spot in Anna's heart. The part that had wished people understood how grief came in unexpected waves sometimes, how it followed its own timetable. To her horror, her eyes welled with grateful tears. She clumsily shifted her grip on Matthew to free one hand and dashed them away.

"I'm sorry," she whispered.

"Don't be. If you'd rather not do this today, I can come back some other time."

"*Nee,*" she said quickly. "That's not necessary. But if you don't mind, why don't you just look the house over for yourself? I'll be on the porch if you have any questions."

Pushing open the screen door with one shoulder, she carried Matthew outside and sank into one of the rocking chairs. She settled her son in her lap, and he yawned again and closed his eyes, going peacefully limp against her.

She rocked him gently—and waited. There was no sound except for the trilling of birds in the trees and the occasional roar of an Englischer's car going past on the road.

And a man's heavy footsteps moving through the house, making the boards upstairs creak as he inspected room after room.

She rested her chin on top of her son's fluffy hair and closed her own eyes. Jeremiah Weaver had surprised her. After what Susie had said about his wedding being called off at the last minute, she'd expected him to be an unpleasant man. Why else would any bride go through the embarrassment and expense of canceling a wedding on such short notice?

Unless maybe the bride was the unpleasant one.

She'd only spent a few minutes with Jeremiah, of course, and maybe he was a stinker, deep down. But so far he seemed like a nice-enough fellow. Kind and gentle…just like old Amos.

Guilt stirred. Susie had kept saying it wasn't her business to worry over who bought the farm, and maybe it wasn't. But she felt bad about selling this farm to any decent fellow without being honest about why she was putting the place on the market in the first place.

But if she did, and if Jeremiah had as much sense as Susie seemed to think he did, he'd never buy a farm, not for any price.

Jeremiah came back downstairs to the kitchen. It hadn't taken him long to see what he needed to see. This place would do. He didn't care much about the house anyway. If he'd had a wife, now…

But he didn't. So, as long as he had a place to sleep and a kitchen to cook some simple meals in, he'd be satisfied. It was the barns and the fields he was most interested in, and those had passed his inspection with flying colors.

Oh, there was work to do, a sight of it, like he'd told Anna. Everywhere he'd looked, he'd seen something else that needed fixing or tidying up.

That part hadn't bothered him. None of the problems he'd seen went deep. The Speicher farm's bones were sound. Good, fertile fields, sturdy buildings, a water source that wouldn't run dry every summer.

It was everything he'd dreamed about, and more.

That was what worried him. His twenty-eight years of life had taught him a hard lesson about what happened when a man reached for more than he was meant to have. The bottom line was, this place was too *gut* for him, and the idea of trying for it made him a little *naerfich*.

But one thing was for sure, nobody else was doing much with it. Why would anybody let this treasure of a farm sit idle for so long? It made no sense. It seemed a foolish choice, and Anna didn't come across as a foolish sort of a woman.

Then again. He recalled the pained look on her face when she'd come inside the house. She'd gone through a hard time, left like that with a baby and a farm to manage. He'd no business second-guessing her choices—nor anybody else's. He'd made more than his own share of mistakes.

He was a little surprised her family hadn't helped out more, but then he didn't know much about her family. She'd moved in with her mother since her husband's death, that much he knew. And recently, she'd left her *mamm*'s home and started renting a room in Susie's house. He wasn't sure why—Susie hadn't said.

Of course, that was another thing that was none of his business. Whatever her reasons, he should count his blessings that Anna had moved in with Susie. Otherwise, he might not have been the first to hear about this opportunity. A nice place like this would likely have been snapped up quick, but Susie had known he was looking for a farm. She'd tipped him off last week when he'd made his scheduled delivery at the bakery where she worked.

A nice woman, Susie Raber. A big talker, but Jeremiah didn't mind that. He was more of a listener himself, but he liked folks who talked—a man learned a lot that way.

So, every week, he'd let Susie chatter uninterrupted while he unloaded things from his wagon into the bakery's storeroom. Afterward she'd offer him a cup of tea and some day-old cookies. Generally, he accepted.

He didn't stop other places. He'd too much work to get done in a day to linger anywhere long. But he'd made it a habit to sit down for ten minutes or so at the little table in the kitchen of Smucker's Bakery, to eat cookies and listen to Susie's latest news.

So he'd heard about it when Anna had moved in after Susie's last renter, Lilah Troyer, left to marry Eben Miller, the owner of Miller's General Store. Susie hadn't been upset with the change, although she'd liked Lilah real well. In fact, she'd seemed to be looking forward to it—especially because the new girl, Anna, would be bringing her son with her.

"I've never had a little one in the house before," Susie had said happily. "That'll be nice, and Anna's such a sweet girl, too. *Ja*, I believe this is going to work out just fine."

Now that he'd met her, he had to agree. Anna did seem sweet. Pretty, too, with blond hair the color of daffodils and eyes as blue as the summer sky. And her boy was a cute, bright-looking child.

He was sorry the two of them had gone through such trouble. But sorrows came to everybody.

Jeremiah thought, though, that some fellow in her family or her husband's should have stepped up to help her. If he'd had Anna in his charge, this farm wouldn't have been allowed to get in poor shape, and she certain sure wouldn't be talking terms with a stranger out here all by herself.

Not that Anna was doing much talking. Jeremiah glanced uneasily at the envelope he held in his hand, then toward the front of the house. A rocking chair gently creaked as she waited for him to finish looking around. He'd have to go out soon, and she'd expect him to have looked over this paper.

He'd not counted on that. He'd insisted on meeting in person, so they could talk this all through. He should have figured that there'd still be papers and reading involved. There always was when something was important, seemed like.

He opened the envelope and pulled out a sheet of handwritten paper. He stood there, studying it, trying to work out what it said.

It was no use. He could read the thing—he *could* read, in spite of what Barbara's *daed* had hinted to his friends after they'd called off the wedding. The letters just tended to mix themselves up in his head. He couldn't always tell the difference between them—not unless he went slow and careful. Right now he didn't have that much time.

He folded the paper and slid it back into the envelope. No point reading this thing anyhow. He knew what he could afford to offer. Now that he'd seen the place, he'd have to adjust that a little, but still, he had a good idea.

The question was, would he and Anna be on the same page? He sure hoped so. Now it was time to find out.

When he walked out on the porch, Anna was sitting in

one of the rockers, her boy asleep in her arms. She looked up and raised her eyebrows.

"All done checking over the house?"

"I am. It's real nice. In pretty good shape, too. There's a few things that'll want fixing, but not too much."

She nodded warily. "That's good."

"But to be honest, I knew I wanted the place before I ever set foot in the house. It's the land I'm most interested in. I reckon we just need to see if we can come to an agreement about the price."

Anna glanced down at her son and sighed. "Before we talk about money, there's something I need to tell you." She nodded to the chair beside her. "You'd better sit down."

"All right." He lowered himself carefully into the seat. He was too long-legged for a lot of chairs, and this one was no different. His boots were all the way to the porch railing. He shifted cautiously, but the thing seemed sturdy enough. "What is it?"

Anna took a deep breath. "Have you ever farmed before, Jeremiah? Because farming… It's hard."

He wasn't sure if he should be amused or insulted. He went with amused. "Most things worth doing aren't easy. I'm not afraid of hard work."

"I'm not afraid of hard work either, but farming's different. It can be dangerous, too. It might not seem so when you look around, but it is." She smoothed a lock of her son's golden hair. "My husband died in an accident in that field right there." She nodded to the green pasture on the western side of the house.

Jeremiah wasn't sure what to say. He didn't want to seem unfeeling, but surely this woman knew that accidents happened all the time. Farming accidents, buggy accidents, fires. Nobody was immune to such troubles.

"I'm sorry for your loss," he said finally.

"One loss of many. My father-in-law was killed on this farm, too. A different accident, back when my husband was just a teenager. My mother-in-law lost her husband and then lost her son, too. And before that, a *grossdaddi*. Right here, on this property."

Ah. Well. Jeremiah scratched his chin. "That's a hard thing," he conceded quietly.

"It is." She took a deep breath and straightened her shoulders. "Farming's like that. Hard. A man has to push himself night and day to make ends meet. Sooner or later he gets tired and careless, and accidents happen. And that's why I'm selling the farm. I don't want my son to struggle like the other men in his family have done."

Selling the farm? Jeremiah frowned, confused. What was she talking about?

"That's what I wanted you to know," she went on. "I'm willing to sell you this place, if you still want to buy it, assuming we can agree on the price. I just needed to be honest with you about why I'm putting it on the market."

"I don't understand," he said after a second. "You want to sell the farm?"

"I'm not acting like it, am I? But you seem like a decent man, and Susie likes you. I wouldn't have felt right if I didn't tell you that before we talk about price. Although, Susie said if anybody could make a go of the place you could. And—" Her blue eyes skimmed over him. "She might be right. I don't know. I suppose you'll have to find out for yourself. So? Are you still interested in the farm?"

"*Ja*, I'm interested, but—"

"Then all we have to do is settle on an amount. I can come off the price a little, since you mentioned the damages you saw. A little," she repeated anxiously. "I need the money for a business I plan to start, so I can't take much less. What are you willing to give?" She paused. "Or do you need to think that over before you make an offer?"

He didn't need to think anything over. He already knew the answer to her question.

Everything he had.

That's what he was willing to give. Anna wasn't the only one whose feelings got in the way of good business sense. He'd give every penny he had to have a farm like this to call his own, to work on and tend and rebuild. There was only one problem.

But it was—as usual—a big one.

Chapter Two

As she waited for Jeremiah to answer her question, Anna's pulse went faster and faster. She was surprised her pounding heart didn't wake Matthew, but her little son slept on, undisturbed.

Please, Gott.

If Jeremiah bought the farm, this sad chapter of her life would be over. With the money from the sale, she could start building a new life for herself and for Matthew. A better life and hopefully a happy one.

If he didn't...

Well, it wouldn't be the end of the world, but it would mean that there'd be more waiting ahead. More scrimping and pinching, probably more arguments from Henry's brothers about how she shouldn't sell the farm at all but should keep it for Matthew.

And no doubt more proposals, too—and more pressure from Mamm to accept one of them.

At last Jeremiah sighed—a deep sigh that seemed to come from the very soles of his well-worn boots. Anna tensed.

That didn't sound promising.

"You and I have got ourselves a problem," he said. "I'm not ready to buy a farm just yet. I'm only looking to rent one."

"Rent?"

"That's right. I'd pay a certain amount each month, and—"

"I know what it means to rent a place." It was rude to interrupt, but she was too flustered to care. "This farm isn't for rent, only for sale." She frowned, puzzled. "That's all on the paper I gave you." She nodded at the opened envelope lying in his lap.

Jeremiah cleared his throat. "I…uh…didn't read that too careful. I was busy looking over the house. Would you consider it? Renting?"

Anna shook her head. "I don't think so."

"Have you thought about it? It might make *gut* sense for you. If you rent the farm to me, then you'd still own it."

Anna shot him a frustrated look. "I don't want to own it. I explained to you just now why."

"You did, and I understand why you'd feel like you do. Me, though, I feel different. I'd like to own this place. I really would. But maybe it'd be good for you to have more time to think it over before selling it."

"I've already thought about it plenty."

"What about your boy?" He nodded at Matthew sleeping in her arms. "Could be he'll want his *daed*'s farm one day."

"I told you, Matthew's not going to be a farmer."

"*Ja*, you told me, but…" He scratched his jaw. "I know you've been hurt here, and I'm sorry for it. But this is a real *gut* property, Anna. It'd be a fine place for a young man to start out with some day. And farming's in the boy's blood. A man's got to make a living, and it just makes sense, most times, to go into whatever business your family does."

"Exactly." Anna nodded. "And that's why I'm selling this farm. Like I said, I'm planning to start a business myself. Matthew can take that over one day, if he wants to."

She'd planned it all out. She knew everybody expected she'd marry again. Mamm certainly didn't bother to hide her opinions about the matter. Anna suspected that was why her mother had been agreeable to the idea of Anna renting a room from Susie Raber—Susie had a reputation as a matchmaker. Even the bishop had dropped some hints lately, letting it be known that Anna's sorrow had run its course, and it was time for her to consider a new life partner.

He could hint all he wanted. Anna wasn't interested.

"A business?" Jeremiah studied her thoughtfully. "What sort of business, if you don't mind me asking."

Anna hesitated. She'd only discussed her plans with a few people so far, and it felt strange to share them with a man she barely knew. "I want to open a store."

"A store."

"A specialty grocery," she explained. "Selling bulk goods, grains and spices, things like that. I'm a waitress at Yoder's Dinner Bell downtown, and that's where I got the idea. They had a little grocery section there for years, but now that the tourist trade has picked up, they need the space for more restaurant seating. That means nobody's selling such things locally anymore."

"But if the restaurant folks were making *gut* money selling those spices and such, wouldn't they want to keep on with it?" He looked uneasy. "I don't mean to stick my nose in, but—"

"*Nee*, that's all right. It's a smart question. I thought about that myself. I rang up plenty of sales of those things, so I know people wanted them. But for the Yoders, it was just a sideline, and they didn't pay as much attention to it as they could have. They didn't keep well stocked or worry much about how they had things set out on the shelves. And, of course, since they didn't have much space to spare, they only offered a few items."

"But you'd do different."

"I would." She went on to describe her plans—carrying a bigger selection and offering some smaller quantities for Englisch people who didn't need twenty-five-pound bags of wheat berries or oats. She'd stock in nonfood items, too, like grain mills and empty spice bottles, to up her profits.

She'd not expected to share so much, but for some reason she kept talking. Maybe because Jeremiah was listening so closely, his brown eyes intent on her face.

When she finally went quiet, Jeremiah rubbed his jaw again. "Well," he said finally. "You've sure thought this out. Seems like it's a sound idea, and I think you'll likely make out well."

The praise took Anna by surprise, and for a second she didn't know what to say. Nobody else had been optimistic about her plans. Her mother had strongly suggested she keep working for the Yoders while she waited to see what the future held. Clearly, Mamm hoped that before long, Anna would be busy caring for a husband again, maybe more children, and would forget all about opening a store.

"I'm glad you think it sounds smart. But, of course, to start up any business I'll have to have money. That's why I need to sell the farm. Maybe we can still work something out between us, though. Why don't you go ahead and read over that paper? It spells out everything I need to have. I'll wait until you're done, and then we'll talk."

A familiar anxiety stirred in Jeremiah's chest. Him? Read over this whole paper right now? Not likely. He doubted Anna had that much time to sit on this porch.

Besides, although he didn't consider himself a prideful

man, he wasn't eager to have this smart woman—a woman with well-thought-out plans about starting up her own grocery business—watch him sounding out words like a schoolboy.

So, he shook his head. "There's no point. Nothing on this paper changes anything."

She bit her lip. "If you don't have the money for a down payment, maybe—"

"It's not that. I've got money put by." Ever since his plans for a future with Barbara had fallen apart, he'd done little but work and sleep. "But the money was hard-earned, and I want to be careful with it. I'm willing to work hard, but I've never farmed for myself before. I worked on my—" He stopped just in time. He'd started thinking of Samuel Esh as his father-in-law when Barbara had agreed to marry him. And Samuel had encouraged that—too much, as it had turned out.

Jeremiah took a breath and went on more carefully. "I hired out on my neighbor's dairy farm for years, so I know a little something. But I'm not going to run cows. I'm planning to grow produce to supply the local restaurants and markets, and that's new to me. I figure it'd just be foolishness for me to jump in without testing the waters first."

"I see." She sighed. "Well, I know firsthand how hard it is to farm for a living nowadays. Most men around here are getting out of it and moving into other businesses. You're wise to be cautious."

He couldn't fault her answer. It was simple, honest and politely given. But there was a disappointment in her blue eyes that he didn't like one bit. The desire that had been building in him all afternoon, the yearning to throw caution to the wind and just buy this beautiful place outright, grew a little more.

Not because it was a *gut* farm, though it was. Not because he missed the happier days he'd spent working at the Esh dairy, though he did. And not because he'd grown tired of working as a deliveryman for the local businesses, although he had.

But because he'd really like to see Anna's face light up.

A *dumm* reason if there ever was one. It wasn't his job to make Anna Speicher smile. He'd treat her fair, of course, but he had to look after his own interests, too.

That was proving harder than he'd expected. Anna's late husband must have been a strong-minded fellow, Jeremiah reflected ruefully. If he had a woman like Anna for his wife, he'd likely never be able to tell her no about anything.

Good thing there was no danger of Jeremiah facing any such problem. A bright, pretty woman like Anna Speicher would never be satisfied with a husband who could barely puzzle out the labels at the grocery store.

On the other hand, he did know how to fix fences and replace splintered boards—that work he could do as well as anybody. An idea occurred to him.

"Like I said, I want to try my hand at farming before I buy property. But if I do well, this is just the sort of place I'd like to own. How about I rent the farm for one year and see how I do? If I turn a profit, I'll buy the property from you then."

She was shaking her head before he even finished talking. "I'm sorry, but *nee*. I can't do that. Like I explained, I need the money."

"I understand. It would mean waiting another year to start up your business, I guess. But, like I told you, there's plenty around here that needs fixing—mostly small jobs but a few big ones, too. A buyer will have to take that into consideration—the cost of making those repairs. They'll want that much knocked off your asking price, maybe more for the trouble of it. You'd get better money if you put the farm on the market in better shape."

"Maybe I would." A frown puckered Anna's brow. "But I've no money to pay for the materials and nobody to do the labor."

Jeremiah paused, but being honest was more important to him than getting his way. "The men in your church would likely help you fix the place up to sell." Widows were generally well looked after, not only by their immediate family but also by their communities. "And maybe your husband's family would help with the money."

"They would, if I asked." She hesitated. "But I'd rather take care of this myself. My husband's family would like me to keep the farm for Matthew. They don't want the place themselves," she hurried to add. "I asked. They're all settled with businesses of their own. But they're not real happy about me selling it. That's one reason I've waited so long to do it." Her little boy stirred in her lap, and she stroked his arm, settling him.

"Well, if you'll rent it to me, I'll fix everything and pay for the materials out of my own pocket. I know a year seems a long time, but it isn't, really. And you can ask anybody— I'm a good, dependable worker."

She studied him, her head tilted to one side, still stroking her son's small arm. She seemed to be considering it, so he pushed, gently.

"What's the worst thing that can happen? If I can't buy the place at the end of the year, you'll still end up with a well-kept farm that's worth a good bit more than it is right now."

She nodded slowly. "That's true, I guess. But something's worrying me."

"What?"

"This doesn't seem like such a great deal for you, paying for the materials and doing the work on a place you don't even own. Why would you agree to such a thing?"

He'd not expected that question. *Because you have pretty blue eyes, and I feel sorry for you* probably wasn't the right answer to give. Thankfully, there was another answer, just as true and not half so foolish.

"This place suits me better than the others I've looked at, and I'd like a shot at buying it in a year's time. You don't want to rent it, so it's only right for me to sweeten the deal. I'm a fair man, Anna, and I'm honest in my dealings. I can give you some names of folks I've done work for. They'll tell you that I'll live up to my end of any bargain we make together."

Samuel Esh's name wouldn't be on that list, although he'd sure had no complaints for all the years Jeremiah had chored at his dairy. But since the day Jeremiah had walked into the Esh kitchen and told Barbara's parents that the wedding would have to be called off, the Esh family's opinion of Jeremiah's character had taken a nosedive.

Except for Barbara. And she was the one who'd mattered.

Anna's lips pursed into a pout as she considered the offer. "Susie thinks a lot of you," she said finally. "Her opinion counts more with me than what people I don't know might say. How much rent are you able to pay?"

That question he was ready for. Before driving over, he'd come up with a price range he could manage and that matched up with what he'd seen on the rental market. He'd planned to start on the lower end and negotiate up only as far as necessary, but after a second's hesitation, he quoted a price at the top of what he could pay.

Only because this was the best farm he'd looked at, he told himself.

Mostly.

She gazed over the fields as she thought it over. "And you'll really do the repairs that are needed? All of them? Can you make a list for me?"

"I can. It'll take a little time, though." A lot more time than she'd imagine, if she wanted it all written down, but he saw no reason to share that. "I'll want to walk the place over again, to make sure I've caught everything. But *ja*, I'll get you a list."

She nodded, sighed, and scooted to the edge of her seat, preparing to stand up, not so easy to do with the little one in her arms.

"Let me take him." He reached for the boy. "I'll carry him out to your buggy."

She looked startled at the offer, but she allowed him to take the child out of her arms. He settled the boy against his chest. Jeremiah had half expected a fuss, but the little one barely stirred.

"Sound sleeper," he said.

"Like his *daed*." A sad smile flitted over Anna's lips as she gazed at her son. She tilted her head back to look Jeremiah in the eye.

"I'll agree to let you rent the place under the conditions you've given. Along with one of my own."

"What would that be?"

"If you buy the farm at the end of the year, we'll deduct all the rent you've paid and half the cost of the materials from my asking price."

Jeremiah frowned. "You don't have to—"

"*Ja*, I do," she interrupted. "You're not the only one who's fair, Jeremiah. You're still donating your labor and half the material costs, so I'm not coming away empty-handed. Are we agreed?" She stuck out her hand.

He thought of arguing, but the set of her jaw warned him against it. This woman might look delicate and sweet, but she meant what she said. "*Ja.* We are agreed."

He shifted the boy over to one arm and took her hand in his as gently as he could. It was like holding a little bird, fragile and soft.

It had been a while since Jeremiah had held a woman's hand, and by the time he released Anna's, his foolish heart was pounding like a hammer. He turned away quickly and strode down the porch steps and across the yard, carrying Matthew to the buggy. He put the sleeping child carefully in the back seat, then stuttered clumsily through his good-byes, hoping Anna wouldn't notice.

She didn't seem to, but Jeremiah was halfway back to his rented room in Owl Hollow before he was thinking straight again. Although he was usually dog-tired and ready for sleep by day's end, long after he'd gone to bed, he was still awake, thinking over the afternoon, remembering every word he'd said. Remembering the way Anna had tilted her head to look up into his face, and how the summer sunlight had glinted off the gold in her hair.

By the time midnight rolled around, he was disgusted with himself. Something about the woman had made him go even softer in the head than usual.

Gut thing she had no love for that farm. She'd likely not come around there much.

And that, Jeremiah reflected, as he rolled over and tried to quiet his mind for sleep, was definitely for the best.

Chapter Three

❦

"Are you sure you don't mind keeping Matthew, Susie?" Anna asked. "I can take him with me to the farm if that would be easier."

Susie glanced up from the cookie batter she was mixing at the kitchen table. She worked most Saturday mornings, but in the afternoons she liked to try out new recipes for the bakery. "Don't be silly! It'll be much easier for him to stay here with me."

Since they'd moved into Susie's farmhouse, her landlady had often offered to watch Matthew. Although looking after whatever child happened to be handy was a common task for Plain women, Anna tried not to accept too often.

Susie had no children of her own, and this was the first time she'd rented to a woman with a child. Anna didn't want to wear out their welcome. She needed this living arrangement to work out.

It was providential how this room at Susie's had become available right about the time Mamm decided it was time to move into the little *dawdi haus* and let Anna's sister Elizabeth and her husband, Levi, take over the big house.

Of course, Anna and Matthew could have stayed on—everybody had been very clear about that. And she'd considered it, up until the evening she'd overheard Elizabeth and Levi talking over how they planned to settle their growing family into the house.

They'd been discussing which bedrooms would go to which children and which they would keep for themselves.

"And we'll have to keep a bedroom for Anna and Matthew," Elizabeth had said.

"*Ja*, of course." Levi had sighed. "Family is family, and any sister of yours is always welcome. It doesn't seem sensible, though, when you think about it. We're crowding our *kinder* together four to a room when Anna has that whole farmhouse sitting empty."

"I know." Elizabeth's voice grew fainter as she and her husband walked down the hall. "But we'll make do. Anyhow, Mamm says Anna will probably marry again, so it's not likely to be a problem for long."

Afterward, Anna had sat in her bedroom, thinking. Her brother-in-law was right, she'd realized. It was selfish of her to take up space he and Elizabeth needed for their children when she had a perfectly good house of her own. She didn't plan to marry again or bring Matthew up on a farm, but her choices shouldn't make things harder for the rest of her family.

She'd remembered what Mamm had said at lunch—that Susie Raber was looking for a new renter now that Lilah Troyer had married Eben Miller. The next day Anna had gone to the bakery, and she and Susie had fixed it up between them.

Mamm hadn't argued, no doubt hoping Susie would find a match for her stubborn daughter the way she had for the outspoken Lilah. But Anna had wasted no time making it clear to Susie that she wasn't interested in remarrying.

Thankfully, Susie hadn't seemed to mind, and they'd

settled in together very well. Anna glanced around the bright, clean kitchen, smelling pleasantly of vanilla and butter. She already felt at home here, and so did Matthew. This was working out well, and she wanted to keep it so.

"Are you sure?" Anna asked her friend again. "I know you're testing new recipes today, and I don't want him to get in the way."

"Matthew's never in the way." Susie smiled down at the two-year-old, who was sitting in a booster seat at the table eating the raisins she'd set in front of him, one by one. "He's good company, especially on a rainy day." She looked out the window at the overcast day and sighed. Susie didn't like rainy days. Her husband had been killed in a buggy accident during a storm, and bad weather still made her *naerfich*. "Besides," she went on, "I thought you might appreciate a little privacy." The older widow's face softened with understanding sympathy. "Sorting through old memories can be a hard job."

Susie was right. Anna wasn't looking forward to packing up the last few personal belongings that she wanted to take away from the house. Over the past couple of years, she'd sold a lot of things to pay off debts and to cover the yearly property taxes. Most of the remaining items held sentimental value.

But she'd already put the job off for too long, and now she had no choice. Jeremiah had stopped by the restaurant the other day to drop off the first month's rent. She needed to get her things out today because he wanted to move in this coming week.

"I expect I'll manage." She stooped to kiss Matthew on the top of his blond head. "Be a good boy. I'll be home in time to help with supper."

"Take your time," Susie said.

A light rain was falling as Anna drove the buggy to the farm. It persisted as she went through her old home room by room, filling cardboard boxes with various odds and ends. Some things she planned to take with her, either to use or to donate to someone who needed them. The church kept a list of needy folks who were grateful for hand-me-downs. She stacked those near the door, hoping the rain would slack off before she had to carry them to the buggy.

The things she wasn't quite sure what to do with, she carried into the attic. As she arranged the boxes neatly under the eaves, raindrops pattered on the roof.

Henry would have liked this rain, Anna thought sadly. It was a farmer's favorite kind, light but steady. She'd have appreciated it, too, for different reasons. The wet weather would have brought Henry in from the fields early, and it took the edge off the summer heat.

She'd propped the front and back doors open to catch the breeze, just as she would have done then. When she came down from the attic, the house felt pleasantly cool.

Anna didn't feel so pleasant herself, though. She was tired, and her feelings were all jumbled up. Just as Susie had warned, it had been a hard job, emptying drawers and cupboards, some she'd not opened since Henry's death. Memories, good ones and sad ones, had swirled up—along with an embarrassing amount of dust.

She'd give the house a good going over before she left. She wanted to leave the place tidy for Jeremiah.

He seemed a nice man, Jeremiah. A little odd in some ways, maybe, but there was a kindness in him that Anna instinctively trusted. He'd acted strangely flustered just at the last of their first meeting after they'd shook on their deal, but she'd appreciated the gentle way he'd settled Matthew in the buggy. He'd even pulled out the thick blanket that she kept under the back seat for winter drives, padding the buggy floor in case Matthew rolled off.

Ja, a very nice man. Pity he wanted to farm. The poor fellow was in for a hard life. There was nothing she could do about that, but at least she could start him off with a clean house.

But right now she was so tired. Not just physically, but emotionally, too. It wouldn't hurt to sit down for just a minute before she started cleaning.

She sank into her favorite chair and closed her eyes. The rain pattered on, soothing and soft, and a gentle breeze fanned her cheek. She slipped into sleep, dreaming of Henry and of happier days.

Jeremiah stood in the back field of the Speicher farm and squinted up at the gray sky, breathing in rain-scented air. No sign of this weather changing anytime soon. He didn't mind getting wet, but maybe he'd better start walking back to the house. There was one last outbuilding he wanted to look over. Then he'd be ready to make that list Anna had asked for.

When he'd arrived at the farm an hour ago, Anna's buggy had been parked in the yard, and her horse was in a stall in the barn. No doubt she was inside the house, finishing the last of that packing she'd mentioned.

He'd hesitated, wondering if he should let her know he was here, maybe offer his help. There might be heavy items to carry, and she'd brought a buggy, not a wagon. Could be everything she wanted to take wouldn't fit. He could drive the rest of it over to Susie's or wherever she might want it taken.

But after thinking it over, he'd turned away and headed across the fields. Best he left her in peace. Couldn't be easy, what she was doing today. He'd never lost a wife, only the hope of one, but that had been hard enough, especially since he'd taken all the blame for the broken engagement onto his own shoulders.

It had been better that way—for Barbara, at least—and if he had it to do over again, he'd do the same. But it had meant his weathering his own disappointment without any sympathy or support. The entire Owl Hollow Plain Community had sided with the Esh family. Even his own *mamm*— she'd still been living then, but sickly already—had been grieved and ashamed.

And it took a lot to shame his *mamm*. She'd been married to a Weaver. She was well used to embarrassment. He'd have liked to explain things to her, but he couldn't—not without causing Barbara trouble. So, he'd held his tongue.

Jeremiah understood how people felt. He knew what it looked like. The Weavers had a reputation for being shift-less. He'd been the one exception, and people credited Samuel Esh for Jeremiah's good character. The way Owl Hollow saw it, Samuel had taken a fatherless boy under his wing, given him a job, agreed for him to marry his daughter— and look how Jeremiah had repaid him.

Ja, that had been very hard, but it still didn't compare to what Anna had gone through. So, he'd leave her be. When he came back, if she was still here, he'd check in, see if there was anything he could do. In the meantime, he had his own business to attend to.

Even though today had been all about checking for dam-ages and problems, Jeremiah's walk in the rain had only fueled his determination to own this farm. In fact, he was fighting an urge to march into the house and tell Anna that he'd changed his mind. He'd forget about waiting a year and buy the property, right now.

She'd like that, he reckoned. She'd probably smile at him—and he lost several seconds imagining how her face would look when she did. How her blue eyes might sparkle, with the sadness washed out of them.

Jeremiah realized he was standing still in the rain, staring into space as if he'd lost his *gut* sense. He snorted and started walking again, his boots sinking into the rain-softened ground, thoroughly disgusted with himself.

That right there—his having such silly thoughts about a woman he barely knew and who wouldn't have looked twice at him if they weren't doing business together—that was exactly why he needed to stick to his original plan. Maybe he wasn't a *schmaert* man, at least not in the ways most people counted it, but he had enough common sense to make up for his weaknesses.

Usually.

When it came to a big decision, he'd learned to take his time. He thought things through, asked the advice of folks he trusted. Most important, he tried to be realistic about his own abilities, which—like it or not—weren't the same as other people's.

Because when a fellow forgot such things and aimed too high, life had some harsh ways of reminding him. Like finding a sweet girl crying her eyes out behind the barn over being pressured into marrying a man she couldn't love, just because her *daed* had no sons and needed a strong back and free labor.

That was an experience he'd just as soon never repeat.

He believed he could manage a farm. Farming was mostly physical work, and that was work he knew how to do—and could do well.

But he couldn't be certain, so he'd work this farm for a year, and see how things went. If he turned a profit at it, then—and only then—would he buy the place and settle down.

Jeremiah cut behind the barn, heading toward the small building close to the road that he wanted to check. It looked fairly sound, but he hadn't been inside yet. He'd take a look around and make mental notes of anything needing attention. Then he'd talk to Anna and go over what he'd found.

She'd asked him for a written-out list, but he was hoping to find a way around that. He could write everything down, of course, but that would take a long time, and he wasn't sure he'd spell everything right. He was better at talking.

He'd casually suggest that she make the list herself while he told her what he'd found. If he was a little sly about it, likely she wouldn't even notice that he'd gotten her to do the writing for him. He could just—

He stopped, one hand on the wooden door of the building. listening. Something was scuffling around inside.

No telling what. Could be squirrels or a possum. A raccoon, maybe. Such animals often moved into empty buildings. They sometimes did considerable damage, too.

The small building had been built with plenty of good-sized windows, important for Plain people who relied on sunlight and lamplight for working. He leaned forward to peer through one beside the door, but the afternoon was dim because of the overcast sky, and the inside of the building was dark. He couldn't see much.

He went back to the door, pushed it open slowly and stepped inside. As he did, whatever it was scrabbled in the far corner. He took a step in that direction and was rewarded with a startled yelp—followed by a whine.

A dog crouched, trembling, under a few boards leaning against the wall. Jeremiah bent to get a better look.

It was a scruffy, medium-sized female dog, not too old

and way too thin. He couldn't tell what color her coat was, but it didn't look wet, so it had been in here for a while.

He frowned. The door had been shut tight. He glanced around. There was no other door that he could see.

"How'd you get in here? Stop all that shaking. I'm not going to hurt you." He clucked his tongue and patted his pants leg. "Come out and let me get a better look at you."

As if she'd understood him, the dog lowered her belly to the ground and crawled forward, whining, her eyes rolled up pleadingly. Jeremiah stayed where he was, not moving until the animal was well within reach. Then slowly he extended a hand, fingers folded in, for the dog to sniff.

One sniff did the trick. The dog began licking Jeremiah's hand, whimpering, her tail wagging.

Jeremiah soothed and patted while he gave the animal a quick look over. She was barely more than a pup, and skinny. Her ribs stood out in hard lines under a dirty coat that looked to be at least three or four different colors.

"Poor girl," he muttered. "What no-good rascal shut you in here with nothing to eat or drink?"

No telling. This building was close to the road, and it had been left unlocked. Nobody had been living on the farm for a while, so apparently somebody had decided it was a convenient place to dump off an unwanted dog.

And leave her to starve or thirst to death. Jeremiah tightened his lips and stood.

The dog watched him, fear and hope battling in her brown eyes.

Why not? Every farm needed a good dog.

"You looking for a job? Doesn't pay much, but you'll get room and board." The dog's pointed ears quivered as she listened intently. She barked, and he chuckled. "Come on, then."

He scooped her up in his arms and elbowed his way back out into the rain. He'd carry her back to the house. Maybe Anna had left something in her kitchen that a hungry dog could eat.

He went to the back door and found it ajar, only the screen door in place. He was about to call out, when he caught sight of Anna.

She was asleep in a chair in the living room. Her face was turned toward him, and her eyes were closed. Her *kapp* had slid slightly out of place, and her golden-blond hair glowed in the dimness of the room. She was breathing slowly and deeply, a sweet smile on her lips.

She looked so peaceful—and so exhausted—that he hated to disturb her. He eased the screen door open and shut it as quietly as he could. Then he glanced at the kitchen cupboards.

Anna hadn't lived here for three years, he realized. There'd be no food on hand. But she'd said anything that was left in the house was his to use. At least he could give this poor animal a bowl of water. Then he'd wake Anna up and tell her the list of things that needed attention before he left. He could pick up dog food on the drive home.

He set the dog on the floor. "Don't get used to this," he warned in a whisper. "I'm just renting, so you'll have to bunk in the barn." She wagged her tail.

He opened and closed cupboards as quietly as he could, looking for a bowl while the dog explored the kitchen. He kept an eye on the animal, but since there didn't seem much she could get into, he let her be.

He finally located a small metal bowl and went to the sink to fill it. As he did, he noticed that the dog had discovered a small stack of cardboard boxes beside the back door. Anna's things, no doubt, that she planned to take with her today. The dog reared up on her back legs to sniff them over, and the top box teetered dangerously.

Jeremiah jumped to catch the box, dropping the bowl, which clanged noisily on the floor. The dog bolted to the living room, her toenails clattering over the wooden planks.

The noise startled Anna awake. She blinked, scrubbing at her face with the sleeve of her lavender dress. Jeremiah sighed. He'd better start apologizing.

But Anna spoke before he could.

"You're back early," she murmured, yawning. "Is it suppertime already?"

Jeremiah stood frozen as Anna's eyes, blurred with sleep, met his. For a second, she looked bewildered.

Then, to his horror, her face crumpled into tears.

Chapter Four

The feelings Anna had pushed aside all day rose up in a wave and crashed over her in an unexpected flood. She buried her face in her hands and sobbed. She was dimly aware of Jeremiah hovering nearby, but that only made her cry harder. She wished he'd go away.

She didn't want this—any of it.

She'd tried to accept Gott's will in Henry's death. Most days she felt like she had, but today...today was hard. She didn't want to be here, in her old home, sorting through the broken bits of her former life. And she certain sure didn't want to break down in front of a man she barely knew.

She just couldn't help it.

She'd been dreaming, a sweet, gentle dream of happier days, the last ones of her marriage. Back then, she'd been extra tired because of her new pregnancy. Often she'd sat down in the living room, intending to focus on some sewing, or maybe write a letter, and instead had fallen fast asleep. Henry had woken her up more than once, coming in from the fields, making clumsy man-noises in the kitchen. Jeremiah must have done the same, and somehow she'd worked the familiar sounds into her dream.

Waking up to find not Henry but Jeremiah looking down at her had startled her, and she'd lost the tight grip she'd kept on her emotions. Now she inhaled shuddering breaths, struggling to get her feelings back under control.

"I'm so sorry," she managed. "I don't—I don't know—"

The warm, heavy weight of his hand dropped onto her shoulder. She glanced up, the outline of Jeremiah's face blurred by her tears.

"Nee," he said quietly. "There's no need for that—for apologies." He looked down at her—his head was only about a foot or so from the ceiling—and gave her shoulder a clumsy pat. "Today's been too hard for you, that's all. Sit there for a minute." He disappeared into the kitchen, and again she heard the sounds of her cupboards being opened and shut. Then a few clinks and the sound of running water.

She didn't know what he was doing—but it didn't matter. It gave her some time to pull herself together.

She drew a few deep, measured breaths. Then she rose to her feet, straightened her *kapp* and quickly scrubbed her hands across her face. She sniffed—and frowned, puzzled. She sniffed again.

She smelled a dog. A very wet dog.

She looked down and, sure enough, muddy paw prints marked a path across the floor, leading to the small closet under the stairs. Its door was ajar.

"Jeremiah? Did you… Is there a dog in the house?" she called.

A brief silence, followed by the sound of heavy footsteps. Jeremiah reappeared in the doorway, looking guilty.

"Ja, there's a dog. I found a stray shut up in that outbuilding closest to the road. Somebody must have dumped her."

Anna gasped, distracted from her own troubles. "How cruel! Nobody's lived on this property for years. My brothers-in-law mow the grass and check on things, but weeks go by between their visits, and they don't look in all the buildings. She'd have died if you hadn't found her."

"She hadn't been there too long, I think. Just long enough to be pretty thankful to see me. I brought her in to see if I could find something to feed her and lost track of her in all the...uh...commotion." He scanned the room. "Where'd she go?"

Anna pointed wordlessly at the trail leading to the closet.

Jeremiah winced. "I'll clean the floor." He chewed on his lip, studying the half-open door. "We'll leave her be," he decided. "She's spooked now, but she'll likely come around. She was real friendly before." A low whistle hummed behind him. "That'll be the kettle." He vanished back into the kitchen.

Anna threw an uncertain glance toward the closet. Spooked or not, the dog apparently needed a bath, and she might not be housetrained, either. But, Anna reminded herself, that was Jeremiah's problem. Whatever mess the dog made, cleaning up after her would be his business.

She walked into the kitchen and found Jeremiah pouring boiling water into two of her old mugs. The strings of tea bags hung over the sides.

He glanced up. "I saw the box of tea in the cupboard when I was looking for a bowl. My *grossmammi* always said that there weren't many troubles that a hot cup of tea couldn't help with." He finished pouring and returned the pot to the stove.

Anna tried to remember when she'd last cooked here. A long time ago. She was surprised the stove had worked. "You'll probably need to get more propane," she said. "Soon, I expect."

"I'll see to it." He pulled a chair out. "Sit."

Anna accepted the seat, and Jeremiah placed one of the

mugs in front of her. It was strange having someone playing host to her in her own kitchen.

"Best let it sit a minute," he suggested gruffly. "Otherwise you'll taste little but hot water. I'm sorry I've nothing
to offer you with it."

Anna felt tears threatening again. After Henry's death,
people's unexpected small kindnesses had made her cry
more often than anything else. And there was something…
touching…about this big man, his shirt damp with rain,
worrying over making her tea, offering comfort as best
he could.

"Just a minute." She went to the living room and rum-
maged in her tote bag. She returned to the table carrying
the container of cookies she'd brought from Susie's.

When she cracked open the lid, the rich smell of molasses filled the air. "Susie made these to take by the school
today, and she had plenty left over." She sat down and
nudged the tin in his direction.

Jeremiah smiled. "Molasses cookies are my favorite."

"Help yourself." As she spoke, she heard a noise behind her.

The dog had emerged from the closet. She watched them
from the kitchen doorway, trembling like a leaf.

"The poor thing!" The dog was far too skinny, and her
fur was dirty and matted. Anna started to get up, but to
her astonishment, Jeremiah reached across the table and
caught her forearm, holding her still.

"Nee," he murmured. "I don't know this dog yet. I
shouldn't have brought her into the house. She acted
friendly enough outside, but she's *naerfich* now, and she
might snap at you. Give her a minute to settle. If she needs
dealing with, I'll take care of it."

"Oh!" Anna sank back into her chair. "All right."

It was a perfectly sensible thing for him to say, but there was nothing sensible about how Jeremiah's warning made her feel. She felt flustered. There was something strangely familiar about this. Sitting at the table in her kitchen with a man, the smell of tea and cookies in the air—and the old, comforting sense of being protected.

She looked down at Jeremiah's calloused fingers, still closed gently over her arm.

Maybe she wasn't the only one flustered because Jeremiah suddenly seemed to realize he hadn't let go. His cheeks turned the color of brick, and he yanked his hand away.

"Sorry," he muttered.

Anna pretended she didn't hear, reaching out to take a cookie. "Let's have our snack. Maybe she'll come over when she sees us eating."

Sure enough, the dog took a few steps forward and whined, her eyes fixed on the cookie.

"She's hungry." Moving slowly, Anna placed the cookie on the floor. Then she scooted it in the dog's direction.

The dog snatched the treat and gobbled it up. After sniffing the floor for crumbs, she took another few steps into the kitchen and barked, softly. When Anna looked in her direction, she wagged her tail hopefully, and twitched her little, pointed ears.

Anna's heart melted. "She's a sunny-natured little thing, isn't she? Even after all she's been through. She wants another cookie. That's all right, isn't it? I'm sure cookies aren't supposed to be part of a dog's diet, but she seems really hungry."

"I don't think a few cookies will hurt her, but we shouldn't take all your food. I'll buy her some dog food on my way home this afternoon."

This little stray had found herself a home. Anna smiled.

"I brought plenty to share." She sent another cookie sliding in the dog's direction. "Susie's always trying out some recipe or another, so there are usually extra goodies around."

"Denki." Jeremiah took a cookie out of the tin. "Susie shared treats with me, too, when I stopped at the bakery with deliveries. They were always welcome. A bachelor's diet gets pretty plain."

He smiled, and Anna felt her lips tip up in response. Jeremiah wasn't what you'd call a handsome fellow. Nice-enough looking and, of course, real strong-built. But the man certain sure did have a nice smile. It changed his face, made him look gentler, and warmed up his eyes.

Anna blinked, startled at the direction her thoughts had taken. Silly to be thinking about a fellow's smile just because he'd made her a cup of tea.

After catching her blubbering like a baby.

Jeremiah was being very nice, but no doubt this was awkward for him. Henry had always been uncomfortable when she cried and unsure what to say.

"I think I do owe you an apology." She picked up one of the spoons he'd set on the table and gently pressed her tea bag before removing it from the cup. "For crying like that before. I'm not… I don't usually behave that way."

He shook his head. "You owe me nothing. I'm sorry I woke you, bringing the dog into the house and making such a racket. No wonder you were upset."

"It wasn't that. It's just…" She managed a half laugh. "I thought you were my husband."

"Vass?" Jeremiah looked as if she'd poked him with a stick. He'd frozen, his mug halfway to his mouth, staring at her.

"Only for a second," she hurried to explain. "I was dreaming. I guess I heard you come in the kitchen like Henry used to, and somehow—"

"You don't have to explain." Jeremiah sounded determined—and a little desperate. "Today was a hard day. You were overtired."

"That's so," Anna agreed, dropping her gaze to her tea mug. She'd embarrassed him, talking so free. She'd not meant to.

"Anna?"

She looked up. *"Ja?"*

"Don't fret yourself. It's all right." His expression was a mixture of sympathy and determination. "You're going to be all right."

People had told her that a thousand times since Henry's death. *It'll be all right, Anna. You'll see. Gott knows best. Everything will be all right.* But nobody, not even Charley Coblentz, their faithful, good-hearted bishop, had ever sounded quite as certain as Jeremiah did.

"Oh, *ja*," she agreed lightly, although she wasn't near so sure as he seemed to be. "Things will be better, especially once I have the store. Then, I won't have time to sit around crying, ain't so?" She managed a laugh. "I'll have too much else to do."

"When will that be?" He frowned. "I've pushed your plans back, renting this farm instead of buying it."

She shrugged, but there was no denying it. "That's so, *ja*. I've a little money put by, but not enough to both rent a place and stock the shelves. I'll just have to be patient, I guess."

He studied her, his brow creased. "I'm sorry."

"It's not your fault. Besides, the arrangement we've made between us is a real *schmaert* one for me. Everybody I talked to said so. It'll be much easier to sell the farm at the end of the year once you've fixed everything. And, of course, you may end up buying it yourself. If you're still interested in farming by then."

She almost hoped he wouldn't be. The more she got to know Jeremiah, the less she liked the idea of him struggling to make ends meet, the way Henry had done, losing sleep over the weather and market prices and such. But, of course, that wasn't her choice to make.

"And I've my job at Yoder's Dinner Bell yet," she added. "I'm thankful for that."

"Do you like working there?"

Anna hesitated. "It can be hard sometimes, but I expect that's good for me. You know what they say. Hard times build good character. Like your sunny little dog there." She nodded toward the animal, who was lying on the floor, her nose on her paws, watching the two of them. "She'll likely be the most loyal dog you'll ever have, because she'll remember her hard times. She'll never forget your kindness."

Jeremiah took a long drink of tea before he spoke.

"Maybe you're right. She does seem to be a cheerful little thing. Sunny-natured, like you said. Looks like you've saved me from having to come up with a name for her. Sunny's a *gut* name for a dog."

Anna smiled. "I like that."

He was glad he'd made her smile. To his way of thinking, Anna had suffered enough hard times already to have a well-built character. Now she had to wait on her store because of him. He didn't like being the cause of that disappointment.

Nee, he didn't like that one bit.

That didn't mean he should do anything about it. At least

not until he'd had time to get off to himself and think things through. He was having trouble right now remembering that Anna Speicher's problems weren't his to solve.

The truth was, his insides had been jumping like a basketful of baby chicks ever since she'd looked up at him with drowsy blue eyes and burst into tears. And that offhand comment she'd made about dreaming he was her husband?

That had nearly finished him off.

His mind—which had often been compared to molasses by his frustrated schoolteacher—had galloped ahead like a snake-spooked horse. In one split second he'd imagined what his life would be like if that were true—if he were Anna's husband, and this was their farm, their house, their little family, together.

That silly idea—and the aching sweetness of the picture it made in his head—had sucked the air right out of the room.

Long story short, this woman tipped him off-balance awful easy, so he'd better be careful.

He cleared his throat. "Mervin Yoder's your boss, ain't so?" She nodded. "I've made deliveries for him a few times." He should have stopped there, but he found himself going on. "He seems to have trouble holding on to his help. Is he hard to work for?"

"Mervin's not a bad man." Anna kept her eyes on her tea. "He's just particular and not always patient when people make mistakes. So, *ja*, he does have some trouble keeping help. Englischers don't stay long at all, and even Plain folks usually move on when they can."

"Why haven't you?"

Anna shrugged, lifting her mug to her lips. "I don't have a choice."

She didn't sound bitter, only resigned. Jeremiah felt

himself slipping sideways, and he scrabbled to hang on to his common sense.

He should drink his tea. He should change the subject and talk about the weather. He should do pretty much anything other than say what he was about to say.

Instead, he said it.

"What if you had a place to open your store now?"

"I explained that. I can't afford—"

"I mean, a place that already belongs to you, that you could use for free." His common sense squawked one last, desperate protest, but he ignored it. "There's that building by the road, the one where I found the dog. I've no plans to use it. Why don't you set up shop there?"

Anna's eyes widened with surprise. Small wonder. He was surprised himself.

"That's generous of you. But *nee*." She shook her head. "I couldn't do that."

"I don't see why not. This farm still belongs to you. No reason why you shouldn't make use of part of it, so long as we're both in agreement."

"It's not that." She set her half-eaten cookie down. "You're being very kind, and I appreciate it. I'm not sure I could bear coming out to this farm every day." She laughed, but there was no joy in the sound. "Not if I fall apart after spending just part of one day here."

Jeremiah weighed the words he wanted to say against the value of minding his own business. "I keep my nose out of other folks' doings as a rule. But if you're willing to hear it, I'd like to say something to you."

Anna hesitated for just a second before nodding. "Of course."

"You should go on and start your store here. It won't be easy, but you can't let that stop you from walking through a door Gott has opened. You'll just have to be stronger than the hard." He shook his head, frustrated with himself. "I'm not saying it too *gut*."

"Nee." Anna was looking at him, a new expression on her face. *"Nee*, I think you're saying it fine. A door Gott has opened." She repeated his words thoughtfully. "Do you think that's what this is?"

"Only one way to find out. Seems to me Gott leads us by some winding roads sometimes. You can't always see too far ahead, so you just have to trust Him and keep walking."

"That's so." She spoke the words softly, almost absently. She looked around the kitchen and sighed. "My life has sure taken its share of unexpected turns, but Gott's always faithful. I should have more courage, for Matthew's sake—and for Henry's. He was a very brave man, my Henry."

"I'm sure he was." Only a brave man, Jeremiah thought, would have asked a girl like Anna Speicher, so pretty and smart, home from a singing. He was sure he'd never have managed such a thing. "But maybe you shouldn't listen to me. I've got no right to offer you advice."

To his surprise, a little smile curved Anna's lips. "You've been very nice to me, Jeremiah. I'd say that gives you the right to speak your mind." She sat in silence for just a minute. Then she gave a short, quick nod and rose to her feet.

"I'll do it," she said. "I'll open my store here. Thank you for the offer." To his surprise, she laid one hand lightly on his arm. "And thank you, too, for your advice. We don't know each other too well, but you have been a real friend to me today, Jeremiah."

He got to his feet. *"Ja*, sure. You're welcome," he said awkwardly.

She smiled, and his heart flipped upside down. "I was

going to sweep out the house and dust it for you before I left, but it's gotten so late…"

"Don't worry about that. I've got to clean up after the dog anyhow. Let me hitch up your buggy. And I'll carry these boxes out for you, too."

After Anna's buggy had rattled onto the road, Jeremiah walked over to take another look at the outbuilding.

The more he looked, the more uneasy he became. Once Anna got a good look at this place, she was likely to be disappointed.

There was a lot of work to do here. The building was filthy and full of odds and ends. There were some boards wanting a nail or two, and it could use a good coat of paint.

Even then, it wouldn't look much like a store. He thought over the businesses he'd made deliveries to over the years. A store wanted shelves. A counter for totting up totals and putting folks' items in bags. Things like that.

None of that was Jeremiah's responsibility, and he had plenty of his own work that needed seeing to. He'd made verbal arrangements with several shopkeepers in the area, promising them produce once his gardens started producing. It was late in the year for putting in warm-weather crops, so he had no time to waste if he wanted to squeeze out a profit this season.

On the other hand, he couldn't work fields in the dark. Maybe after sundown he could knock a few shelves together for Anna. Nothing fancy, just something to help her get started. There were plenty of old boards he could use. Henry Speicher had been thrifty as well as brave. The farm's storage spaces were full of materials that could be repurposed.

Ja, he'd see to it, Jeremiah decided as he walked back out to the fields. Because, as Anna had said, they were friends,

and friends often passed such favors back and forth. Besides, she was a widow in his new community. Like all
Plain men, he'd done plenty of work for widows over the
years. Helping Anna was no different.

Or so he told himself. Although—there was no getting
around it—none of those other widows had a smile half as
sweet as Anna's. None of them had ever made his heart
flip around like a landed fish, either.

He'd better watch his step.

Chapter Five

The following afternoon, Anna turned to her *mamm* and Susie, her heart pounding. "Well? What do you think? I'm planning to call the store the Farmhouse Pantry. I'll stock quality items that Plain women keep on hand and will want to buy in bulk to save money, like grains and spices. But I'll divide some up in pretty little jars and bags so that Englischers can shop here, too."

She'd invited the two women out to look over the store building and get their reaction to her ideas. She'd warned them about the shape it was likely to be in, but when they'd arrived, the place wasn't as big of a mess as she'd expected. The odds and ends Henry had stored here were gone, the floor had been clumsily swept, and she even noted new wood nailed in three different places.

Jeremiah must've worked on this yesterday evening after she'd left. Although she hated the thought of him going to such trouble, she was grateful. Mamm was no fan of this idea, and Anna needed all the help she could get.

Susie stepped inside, glancing around with bright interest. "It's close to the road. That's good."

Anna's *mamm*, Mary Glick, who had Matthew balanced on one hip, poked her head through the door, and wrinkled her nose. "It smells musty, and there's dirt and cobwebs on the walls."

"It needs a good cleaning," Anna admitted.

"Even then it won't be fit for a store. No shelves, no counter. No place for storage." Mary shook her head. "You know how important those things are for such a business, Anna. You remember your father's store, don't you? This is a far cry from that."

Anna cast a desperate glance at Susie, but her friend was looking out of a grimy window and seemed unaware of the conversation behind her.

Anna smothered a sigh. She'd been so excited since her talk with Jeremiah. She'd spent a lot of time imagining how she'd organize her store, how she'd advertise, what she'd stock. She'd barely been able to sleep, she'd been so busy planning. She'd felt tired, but also happier than she could remember being in a long time.

But Mamm's lack of enthusiasm was no surprise. She'd known from the start that her mother wouldn't like this idea. Mamm's plan for Anna's future involved a nice, prosperous husband and several more children—and the sooner, the better. Anna's lack of interest in that hadn't discouraged her mother in the slightest.

Mary settled her grandson more comfortably in her arms. "I don't know, Anna. There's a lot of work to do before you could even think about opening for business. What do you know about running a store anyhow?"

"I helped Daed—"

"*Ja*, exactly. You helped. Your *daed* ran the store." Mary smoothed Matthew's cowlick. "There's a lot more to it when you're in charge. That's why I closed the store after your father passed."

"What do you think, Susie?" Anna held her breath waiting for the answer. Mamm might be willing to listen if Susie thought the store was a *gut* idea.

"What do I think?" Susie turned away from the window and smiled. "I think Matthew is nodding off. Hadn't you better run him back home, Mary, and let him have a nap?"

The distraction worked. Mary's expression softened as she smiled down at her sleepy grandson. "Maybe I'd better. Elizabeth wants me to help her make some blueberry jam before she has to start cleaning the house for church service, so I can't stay away too long."

Homemade blueberry jam. That might be a good addition to the store shelves, and Elizabeth always made more than she could use. Anna opened her mouth to speak, but Susie warned her with a slight shake of her head.

Don't.

"We'll pick up Matthew on our way home," Susie assured Mamm. "And if you still need help with the jam-making, we'll pitch in."

"I'll see you later, then." Mamm sighed. "Try to talk some sense into my *dochder*'s head, Susie."

After her mother carried Matthew out to her buggy, Anna stood silently, her fists wadded into tight balls. Mamm spoke as if Anna was a child who didn't know up from down and couldn't make a smart decision. She'd always tried to be a dutiful and respectful daughter, and she loved Mamm to pieces, she truly did. But honestly...

After Mamm's horse had clopped onto the road, Susie turned to Anna. "Well—" she started.

"This isn't a foolish idea." Anna spoke so firmly that she even surprised herself.

Susie laughed. "*Nee*, it isn't. I think it's a very *gut* idea."

Relief washed over Anna in a happy wave. "Do you really think so, Susie?"

"I wouldn't say so if I didn't, but there's no point arguing with your mother about it just now. Mary has her own ideas, and it'll take her a while to come around. Once this place is scrubbed and fixed up nice, she might be more agreeable. It'll be a sight of work, but that's no problem. We'll make a frolic out of it. Your friends will be happy to roll up their sleeves and help you."

Anna considered. Likely Susie was right. Her friends had been extra compassionate since Henry's death. They would help if she asked them, but that only solved one of her problems.

"Mamm was right about the shelves and such, though. I'll need those things, and my budget's tight. I've no money to stock the store and furnish it both."

Susie waved that worry aside with a careless hand. "That's what the men are for. We've plenty of woodworkers in the community." She wrinkled her brow. "Although that part might not be so quick. Everybody's busy this time of year, and the men will have to fit the extra work in as they can."

"Of course." Anna's blooming hopes wilted a little.

Since Henry's death, she'd been thankful to live in a community where folks looked after each other and took special care of widows. The men in her family and others in the Hickory Springs Plain community had made sure that she and Matthew went without nothing they could provide.

But while her needs were always attended to, that work had to be arranged around the men's personal responsibilities. As grateful as she was—and she was very grateful—it was sometimes a little frustrating to wait for them to find the space to fit in her little tasks.

The sound of a man clearing his throat startled her, and she turned to see Jeremiah looking through the doorway, Sunny at his heels.

She looked like a different dog. She was still skinny, but

she'd had a bath, and someone had combed the mats out of her fur. She didn't seem to enjoy being so close to the building where she'd been trapped, but she looked much perkier than she had before.

Jeremiah didn't look so perky, though. Weary lines creased his face, and he was dusted with a thin layer of brown soil.

He greeted both women with a careful politeness, then turned his attention to Anna. "So? Do you think this building will suit?"

"I think so," she said guiltily. Some of those weary lines were there on her account. "And *denki-shay* for clearing it out for me, and for making the repairs. That was very kind."

"*Ach*, well." He looked uncomfortable. "It needed doing."

"You know," Susie said brightly, "something else needs doing, too. Anna can't very well have a store without some fixtures. She needs shelves and a counter. Could you help with that?"

"Ah," Jeremiah seemed at a loss for words. "Well—"

"Susie!" Anna hissed, mortified. Susie was being awfully pushy. "He won't have time. He's got to get his crops in the ground, or he'll miss the season. Ain't so, Jeremiah?"

"*Ja*, that's so. But as it happens, I—"

"Nobody has much time to spare in the summer," Susie agreed cheerfully. "But she doesn't need anything complicated. If the store does well, she can have custom fixtures built later on. She just needs something to get started. A few rough-built shelves shouldn't take long to knock together."

"*Susie—*" Anna cut in desperately.

Jeremiah spoke at the same time. "I already—"

"Tell you what," Susie interrupted with a smile. "I'll send

you baskets of day-old baked goods, for as long as Anna has her store here. In return, you make her some simple shelves and a counter and help out now and then when she needs something carried or a bit of heavy work done. How does that sound?"

"Susie." Anna spoke with all the sternness she could muster. "Stop pestering. Jeremiah's already done enough, dragging all that junk out of here and fixing the broken wood. He's got a farm to run, and nobody knows better than I do how much work that is. He's got no time for anything else, not when he's planting." She turned to Jeremiah. "Ain't so?"

"The shelves are done. I've been trying to tell you, but I couldn't get a word in edgewise. I nailed together some simple ones last night. Nothing fancy, but they'll get you by. Measured 'em to fit against the walls and around the windows."

Anna and Susie stared, and for a moment even Susie seemed struck speechless.

But only for a moment.

"You made Anna's shelves?" Susie studied Jeremiah, a thoughtful glint in her eyes. "Before we even thought to ask? What a generous thing to do. Ain't so, Anna?"

Anna narrowed her eyes at her landlady. "Very generous," she said. "*Denki*, Jeremiah."

He looked embarrassed. "It needed doing," he repeated. "I'll nail 'em in place once you've got the building scrubbed out. You wouldn't want some Englisch child pulling them over. I don't have a counter made yet, but that won't take long. By the time you've got the place clean, I'll have that ready, too."

"Wonderful!" Susie clapped her hands happily. "We were thinking of having a work frolic to clean the place up. Maybe paint the walls and such. You won't mind that, will you?"

He shook his head. "*Nee*, not so long as you charge the paint to my account at the hardware store."

"I couldn't—" Anna protested quickly.

"It's only right. I promised to see to the repairs and such. You can bring the cleaning supplies, but I'll buy the paint."

"So generous," Susie murmured sweetly. Anna shot her friend another slitted glance.

Jeremiah shifted his weight from one boot to the other. "I'd best be getting back to my work," he said. "*Mach's gut*, Anna. Susie." He beat a hasty retreat, Sunny trotting happily at his heels.

The minute he was out of earshot, Anna put her hands on her hips and prepared to give Susie a piece of her mind.

"Susie Raber! You shouldn't bully that poor man into building my shelves."

"And a counter," Susie reminded her with a wink. "And I didn't have to bully him about the shelves because he'd already built them." She cocked an eyebrow. "I wonder what made him think of doing that?"

Anna's cheeks flamed hot. "I don't know, but he shouldn't have. That poor man already has more than enough on his plate."

"I wouldn't waste much pity on Jeremiah Weaver." Susie walked out into the sunshine and waited while Anna shut the old wooden door. "He's got a strong back, good sense and a willingness to work. Men have done well with a lot less."

"I wasn't criticizing him. He's just very busy, and I just don't like…bothering him."

"He didn't seem too bothered." A smile played around Susie's lips as she led the way across the yard to where her horse and buggy stood waiting. "In fact, if you were in the market for another husband—"

"Nee," Anna said firmly as she hoisted herself into the buggy.

Susie gave her a quick sidelong glance as she settled in her own seat and took up the reins. "Is that *nee* to Jeremiah or still to the idea of marrying again at all?"

Anna glanced toward the field where Jeremiah was plowing. Hot work at midday, but he'd no choice if he wanted to eke out a summer crop. She hoped he'd remembered to stash a water jug somewhere nearby in the shade. Maybe she should have mentioned that, since he'd no *fraw* to remind him of such things.

She turned her eyes away resolutely. Not her place. Jeremiah would have to look after himself.

"Both," she told Susie. "Like I've told you before, I'm not looking for another husband. Even if I was looking, I'd never marry a farmer."

"Pity." Susie guided her mare toward the road. "Jeremiah's a good-hearted fellow and a hard worker, and he sure needs a wife. As for not marrying again," she went on placidly, "you're not the first widow I've heard say such a thing. Most change their minds as time goes by. When that happens, you let me know."

Anna pressed her lips together. She wouldn't argue with Susie. It wasn't polite, and anyhow, there was no point to it. Everybody knew Susie was an incurable matchmaker.

But Anna wouldn't change her mind. Susie would find that out soon enough.

On the morning of the women's work frolic, Jeremiah finished his barn work early. Chock, his brown gelding, was happily crunching his breakfast, and a light rain was pattering overhead. It wasn't heavy enough to keep him out of the fields—not yet—but it might worsen. He needed to get to his work while he still could.

But instead of walking out to the field, he stood in a shaft of gray light, slowly puzzling through a catalog he'd picked up at the feed and seed. He needed to choose some fertilizer and a few other things. He had an idea what he wanted, and he'd like to get it ordered, but this was a lot of reading, and he couldn't afford to buy the wrong thing.

Sunny whined and poked his leg with her nose. He glanced down at the dog and set the catalog down on top of the feed bin where he'd be sure to see it later.

"*Ja*, I know. We've that fencing to see to today, unless we want the deer eating our seedlings as fast as they sprout. But we'd better go speak to Anna first."

The problem of his fertilizer order hadn't been the only thing keeping him in the barn this morning. The truth was, his stomach had gone swimmy at the thought of seeing Anna again today.

She was here already. He'd known exactly when the buggy pulled up, but he'd taken his time finishing up the morning chores. There was no reason why he shouldn't. The barn work was his business. Anna wasn't.

He was still having a considerable amount of trouble remembering that.

Like before, when she'd come out with her *mamm* and Susie Raber. He'd been drawn to the store building like a bee to a blossom. He'd told himself he was just going to check in, to see if there was anything else she needed him to do before he moved the shelves in.

There shouldn't have been. He'd gone over the whole building after he'd removed the junk, picking up spent nails and bits of glass from the floor. He'd repaired some broken trim and even sanded down the windowsill where the wood had broken apart with age. He'd worried her little boy might pick up a splinter running a finger over it.

The place needed a good scrubbing, but he'd left it safe. Still, he'd figured it would be polite to check in with her. He'd let her know about the shelves and then get on with his own work.

Then he'd looked through the doorway and seen Anna standing in a dusty shaft of sunlight coming through the window. She'd looked so sweet and clean and pretty against the grimy walls that it had sucked his breath away.

He wasn't sure he'd even made *gut* sense talking after that, but he'd at least let her know that the shelves were made. He'd made the counter since, working late into the evenings when he'd have been smarter to rest up for his next day's work. He could have gotten through the job a lot quicker, but he'd taken some extra trouble with it.

Which of course, was a poor use of his time—particularly right now when he had so little of it to spare.

It took him a while, but finally when he'd been sanding the wood and sipping his third cup of coffee, he'd figured it out. He wanted to make the counter nice enough that she'd not need to have a better one made later on. He wanted Anna to be impressed by his work. He wanted her to see that he could do things as well as anybody else, at least the things a man did with his hands.

That was pointless and—even worse in Jeremiah's mind—prideful. And more proof that when he looked at Anna Speicher, every drop of *gut* sense drained right out of his head. That had to stop, right now, today, especially since she'd be spending time out here running her store.

He took a breath and walked out of the barn into the misty gray rain, Sunny trotting at his heels. She didn't like the direction he took. She had an understandable dislike of that particular building, but she went along. She was a loyal little thing and would make a fine farm dog, he thought.

Anna's horse and buggy waited outside the store building, tied to an old hitching rail. He tested its sturdiness and frowned. He added replacing the rail to the growing list of chores in his head.

The buggy was crammed with brooms, mops and pails of cleaning supplies. He grabbed a couple of the buckets and walked around to the front of the building.

Anna was inside, holding her little boy in her arms. She turned and smiled when she saw him come in.

"*Gut mariye*, Jeremiah."

Her son blinked at him like a little owl. "Big man," he whispered in Deutsch. Jeremiah grinned at him before turning his attention back to Anna.

"Good morning to you both." He lifted the buckets of supplies he was holding. "Where do you want these put?"

"Oh!" She set the boy down gently and hurried toward him. "*Denki*. Let's see. What's in that bucket? Is it the wood soap or the window cleaner?"

Jeremiah looked down at the buckets in a panic. He wasn't familiar with these products. He'd need to read the labels, and that always took him too long.

"I didn't look," he said shortly. He set the buckets down under the window. "Check it over and see for yourself."

Anna blinked. "Of course. I didn't expect you to unload the buggy. I was about to start bringing everything in myself."

She thought he was being ill-tempered. He started to correct her, then figured maybe he'd best leave well enough alone. At least she hadn't picked up on the fact that he couldn't easily read the writing on the bottles.

"I don't mind hauling the stuff inside," he said gruffly. "I'll let you sort it out."

"All right. I was just taking a minute to plan out what needs doing," she explained.

Plenty, Jeremiah thought, looking around at the dirty walls and the cobwebs. The women had their work cut out for them.

"I'll bring the rest of it in," Jeremiah heard himself offering. "Then I'll unhitch your horse. That rail wants replacing, but I can turn her into the pasture with mine, if that suits. There's shelter for them there if the rain gets bad."

"I know," she reminded him gently.

"*Ach.* Of course you'd know," he muttered, embarrassed.

"So," Anna went on brightly. "Please don't trouble yourself about us. I don't want this frolic to be any bother to you. If you're agreeable, I'll turn the horses into the pasture for the women staying the longest. We'll fill up our scrub buckets at the pump, and I think I've brought everything else we'll need."

"Fine. Make use of the house as you need to, kitchen, bathroom or whatever." He'd spent some extra time this morning doing his best to clean, and he hoped he'd done a decent job. "And let me know when you're ready for the shelves and the counter."

Anna sighed. "I don't expect it'll be before lunchtime. We've got a good bit of cleaning to do, but there's a dozen women coming, so we'll get it done. And then this afternoon, we'll get everything painted."

He nodded. "I'll check with you when I come back to the house to eat. If you need anything before, just give a shout. I'm setting a new fence today, and I'll be working pretty close by."

"You're setting fence? In the rain?" The doubt in Anna's

voice scratched like the blackberry briars he'd been fighting in the back pasture.

"It's only misting, and the ground's good and soft, but not muddy. Should make for fast going. If the weather gets worse, I'll find something else to do."

She considered his words. "I suppose that makes sense. Well, don't let me keep you. Except—I almost forgot. Susie sent you a dozen sausage biscuits. They're in the cooler there." She nodded toward a small red-and-white container set just inside the door. "She said to tell you there'd be plenty more goodies coming your way."

"Thank her for me. I'll carry them to the kitchen and bring the cooler back when I check with you about the shelves." He leaned over to heft it up when Matthew spoke.

"Vi hayst dei puppy?" Anna's son looked up at Jeremiah, one finger in his mouth, the other pointing out the doorway where Sunny waited nervously, her fur dampened by the misty rain.

"You want to know her name? Your *mamm* named her Sunny."

Matthew walked to the door. He looked at Sunny, and the small dog looked back with some interest, leaning forward to sniff. She moved within arm's reach, and the little boy glanced at Jeremiah, a question in his eyes.

"You can pet her," Jeremiah said. "She's friendly. But she'd best stay outside."

"She's welcome to come in out of the rain," Anna said. "She couldn't do any harm in this dirty place."

"Not now, maybe, but later once you've got your store fixed up, you might feel different. Probably best not to start her in bad habits. Anyhow, she doesn't like this place. Bad memories, I guess."

"Ja," Anna said with a sigh. "I can understand that."

They watched as Matthew stuck his chubby arm as far out as he could. Sunny obligingly crept forward so the boy could pet her wet head.

Ach, the dog was wet. Jeremiah cast an uncertain look back at Anna. Women often fussed about such things. But she didn't look upset, only sad. She was rubbing her arms as if she was cold, but it was a warm summer day, even with the rain.

Being here on the farm bothered her, he realized, but she was trying not to show it—trying not even to feel it.

"It's a *gut* thing you're doing." The words came out before he could stop them. "A brave thing, starting up a business all on your own for you and your boy. Plenty *schmaert*, too."

"Oh!" She looked shyly pleased, but he shouldn't have made such a personal comment. She didn't seem to know what to say. "Well—"

They were saved by the rattle of a buggy rolling into the yard, followed quickly by another.

He shot a grateful look through the open doorway. "Your help's here. I might as well see if they want me to unhitch their horses while I'm seeing to yours." He picked up the cooler and stepped around Matthew, through the doorway. "I'll check back with you around lunchtime."

His offer to turn the horses into the pasture was quickly accepted. The women tried talking to him, but he hadn't done so well with that.

He hoped they hadn't thought him rude. The truth was, he couldn't have made small talk right now if his life had depended on it. He kept remembering the change in Anna's face when he'd called her brave—the soft sparkle that had replaced the sadness in her eyes. How she'd held herself a little straighter.

His words had pleased her. And that pleased him—more

than it should've done. Because Anna Speicher's happiness, he reminded himself for the thousandth time, was none of his concern.

He turned the last horse into the pasture and whistled to Sunny, who was sniffing hopefully at the cooler. She smelled biscuits.

Jeremiah, on the other hand, smelled trouble. And in spite of his best efforts, he kept steering straight toward it.

Chapter Six

Paintbrush in hand, Anna climbed down the stepladder and surveyed the room with satisfaction. Today's work frolic had gone well.

The store building sparkled in the late afternoon sunshine. New shelves, wide and deep, lined the walls—more shelves even than she'd expected. Everything shone with fresh paint, and the windows and door were open to allow fresh air to combat the fumes.

True to his word, Jeremiah had come back around lunchtime. They'd scrubbed all the morning, and had the walls cleaned and ready, so he'd brought the shelves in and fastened them down. He'd brought in the counter, too, and it was real nice as well, far nicer than she'd expected.

Overall, she was very pleased. The whole place looked a lot better, and—she sniffed—smelled better, too. The musty odor was gone, replaced by the happier scents of paint, freshly sawn wood and lemon cleanser.

A dozen women milled around her, finishing up the last touches. Just as Susie had predicted, her friends had been happy to help. They'd descended on Jeremiah's farm this morning, their buggies packed with cleaning rags and brushes, cheerful, chatty and full of energy.

They'd descended on Jeremiah, too. A new bachelor in

town was always interesting—almost every woman present had at least one spinster relative looking for a husband.

Jeremiah seemed uncomfortable with all the attention. He'd kept his head down, finished unloading Anna's supplies, nodded to the women and helped them with their buggies. Right after lunch, he'd reappeared and moved in the fixtures, hoisting the heavy shelves up as if they weighed no more than a feather.

After he'd finished putting everything in place, he'd repeated his offer for the women to make free use of the house. He planned to be working on the pasture just behind the barn, he said, so he'd be handy if they needed anything.

Before Anna could thank him, Trudy Schwartz had spoken up.

"That's very generous of you," she'd said. "You're Jeremiah, ain't so? I appreciated your help with my horse this morning." She'd offered her own name and a friendly smile.

Jeremiah had mumbled something polite and beat a hasty retreat, leaving Trudy with a disappointed look on her face. Trudy was in her late twenties and had never been married. Everyone knew she was losing hope of finding a husband.

Anna glanced over at Trudy, who now, like the rest of the helpers, was busy stowing her own cleaning supplies in a bucket for easy carrying. While the other women had worn old clothes, knowing they were likely to get dirty and splattered with paint, Trudy's green dress looked almost new. And it set off her dark hair and matched her eyes.

Trudy caught her looking and smiled. "This is going to be a *wunderbarr* store, Anna. I'm sure you'll do well, and I'm so happy for you."

"That's nice of you to say, Trudy." Anna felt ashamed. Trudy was a sweet person, and Anna could hardly fault any woman for wanting a family of her own. Naturally, she'd be interested in Jeremiah. Anna should be wishing her well, not silently criticizing her. "I'm grateful for your help today."

"I was glad to do it." The other woman leaned in closer. "I admit, I also wanted to get a close-up look at this Jeremiah fellow. He seems nice enough, but not too friendly, ain't so?"

"I think he's a little shy," Anna hedged. "This is a lot of women for any fellow to deal with all at once."

"I suppose so." Trudy's eyes brightened. "If he's shy around women, that might account for him still being single. Although, he almost was married once. I heard the wedding was called off at the last minute. Do you know anything about that?"

"No more than you do."

Trudy looked out the window toward the back pasture. Jeremiah had just finished helping the women hitch their horses to the various buggies and had returned to his fencing. For some reason, he was setting a second fence a few feet out from the original one encircling the field where he was planting his summer crops. Anna had never seen that done before, and it seemed a very silly thing to do.

The two women watched him silently for a second or two as he raised a metal post driver over his head, then brought it down, ramming the new post deep into the ground.

Anna had watched fences being set countless times, but she'd never seen anyone do it so easily. Henry had always struggled with the job and come into the house bone-tired, but Jeremiah had the post in place with three blows.

"My goodness." Trudy slanted a teasing glance Anna's way.

"*Ja*, he's a *gut* worker," Anna said shortly, although she knew that wasn't all Trudy was admiring. As Jeremiah started on the next post, the muscles under his shirt rippled.

"He sure seems to be." Smiling, Trudy turned away from

the window. "I might be stopping in your store often, Anna, and I doubt I'll be the only one. Oh!" She paused, looking uncertain. "I didn't think. Maybe—"

"Maybe what?"

"Maybe you'd rather other women didn't…um…shop here too much," Trudy said, blushing.

It took Anna a minute to figure out that Trudy was hinting Anna might be interested in Jeremiah herself. "You shop all you want," she said.

"Trudy?" Lydia Riehl called from the doorway. The two women had driven over together. "Are you ready? I've got my things loaded in the buggy."

"Coming!" Trudy winked at Anna. "In that case, let me know when you open the store. I'll be your first customer!"

"See there?" Susie Raber, the last of the helpers to leave, paused beside Anna, her cheerful face splattered with tiny specks of white paint. "You've already got folks just waiting for you to open. You're going to have trouble keeping stock on your shelves!"

"I'm afraid spices and bulk goods aren't what Trudy's interested in. She's shopping for a husband. If Jeremiah doesn't look out, he might be a married man before Christmas." Anna forced a smile.

Susie sighed. "I doubt that. Trudy's a sweet girl, but she's got it backward. Men like Jeremiah don't like to be chased. It just makes 'em run all the faster. Not that it matters. Those two wouldn't make a good match, anyhow."

"I don't think Trudy's too picky at this point."

"She should be. An unhappy marriage is far worse than no marriage at all."

The certainty—and the sadness—in Susie's voice caught Anna's attention. She wondered—was it possible that her friend's marriage hadn't been as happy as Anna had always assumed? She wasn't sure what to say, and she was relieved when Jeremiah appeared in the open doorway, putting an end to their conversation.

"Figured you were about to leave," he said. "So I thought I'd come by and see if you needed anything else done." He looked around the room. "Doesn't look like it. Seems you're all set up except for putting out your stock."

"I'll be thankful when that job's done," Susie said with a smile. "Anna's been ordering in her supplies for the past week, and I've boxes and buckets piled to the rafters at my house. Of course, it's going to be a job getting them over here, and some of that stuff's heavy." She cast a thoughtful look at Jeremiah. "I wonder—"

"I can manage," Anna interrupted desperately. The last thing she needed was Susie pestering Jeremiah for more help.

But as usual, Susie paid her objection no attention.

"Maybe, but it would be a lot simpler if Jeremiah would help out with his delivery wagon. You could do that, couldn't you? That way it would only take one trip, and Anna could open her store that much faster." Susie smiled. "If you're done in the fields for the day, Jeremiah, why don't you go get your wagon hitched up? Anna will ride with you and show you where we live, and I'll send you home with another cooler full of food for your trouble."

An hour and a half later, Jeremiah carried the last box down Susie's back steps and stowed it in his delivery wagon with the rest of the store goods. He climbed into the wagon and glanced over at Anna.

"All set?"

"*Ja*, I'm ready." She offered him a strained smile. She

looked nearly as *ferhoodled* as he was feeling himself. He still wasn't sure exactly how this had happened.

He'd planned to stop by the store building for just a minute. Only, he'd told himself, to be polite and to make sure Anna was satisfied with the shelves and the counter. And then before he knew it, he was on a buggy ride alone with a woman for the first time in…well.

Longer than he could remember.

It wasn't going too well. He'd never been a good small talker with girls, but he must be even more out of practice than he'd thought. Their ride over here had been awkward and mostly silent. Next to Anna, who still looked remarkably neat after a hard day's work, he'd felt grimy, gigantic and clumsy, and so self-conscious that he hadn't come up with a single sensible sentence to say.

Anna hadn't said much, either. No doubt she was anxious for this ordeal to be over with, so he'd best get the buggy rolling.

He started to release the brake when Susie hurried out of the house, a container in her hands. Matthew tagged along behind her, his shoulders slumped.

Susie came to the side of the wagon and lifted up the container. "Your goodies," she explained breathlessly. "To thank you for helping today. I almost forgot to give them to you!"

"Denki." He set the tin on the seat between himself and Anna.

There was plenty of room—he could've fit half a dozen tins between them. She'd perched on the farthest edge of the seat, her cheeks as pink as the roses tangled on Susie's fence. Anna was sitting rigidly straight, her small hands folded in her lap.

Small, clean hands, in spite of the day she'd spent painting and cleaning. That made him even more self-conscious of his own thick and not-so-clean fingers. He'd only done a quick wash-up at the pump after finishing the fencing.

"Mamm go?" Matthew gazed up, an untasted cookie clutched in one chubby hand. His face was woebegone, and he looked as if he wanted to cry.

Poor kid. "Don't worry. Your *mamm* will be back home real soon."

The child nodded sadly. When Susie tugged his arm, he obediently stepped back from the wagon, but he didn't smile.

As the buggy rolled down Susie's driveway, Jeremiah pondered the unhappy expression on the child's face.

"Your little one looks unhappy," he said to Anna. *"Vass is letz?"*

"Nothing's wrong," Anna answered. "Not really. He's just used to being with me whenever I'm not working, and he's disappointed that I wouldn't let him come with us."

"Why couldn't he come?"

Anna looked surprised at the question. "Well, you're probably not so used to having children underfoot, and I didn't want him to be a bother."

Jeremiah reined in the horse, slowing the wagon to a stop. "Your boy's no bother. He can ride along, easy as not. If," he added, "that's all right with you."

"Are you sure?" Anna's face brightened.

"*Ja*, of course." He set the brake and jumped down just as Susie and Matthew were starting up the steps to the house.

"Hey!" he called. "Matthew, want to *kumm* with us?"

"Oh, but—" Susie started a protest, but Matthew was already halfway to the buggy.

The little boy stumbled to a stop about three feet in front of Jeremiah, his face a mixture of hope and uncertainty.

"I'll lift you up in the buggy to sit with your *mamm*. *Ja?*" Jeremiah waited for the child's nod before picking him up. The boy felt light as a feather and incredibly small. Jeremiah set him carefully on the seat next to the cookie tin, then swung up to sit beside him.

Anna smoothed Matthew's clothes quickly and put her left arm around him, snugging him close to her side. "Say thank you," she reminded her son.

"*Denki*, big man," Matthew chirped.

"His name is Jeremiah," his mother reminded him sternly, but Jeremiah could hear a smile hiding behind the words.

The boy had just taken a big bite of his cookie, but he obediently mumbled, "*Denki*, Jer'miah," around the mouthful.

"*Du bisht welkomm.*" Jeremiah released the brake and flicked the reins. "Get up, Chock," he ordered the horse.

"Chock?" Matthew laughed, a happy bubbly sound. Plainly, the child thought that was a silly name for a horse.

"It's short for Chocolate," Jeremiah explained. "Because he's the same color."

Serious nods. "I like choc'let."

"Me, too." Jeremiah grinned. At least the ride back to the farm would be interesting—and not so silent. He glanced over at Anna, hoping she was feeling more comfortable, too.

That was a mistake.

She was gazing at her son, a little smile playing around her lips, her eyes full of affection. When she looked up at Jeremiah, the sweetness lingered in her eyes, so pretty and gentle-like that a painful longing hit him square in the stomach like the kick of a horse's hoof.

He forced himself to look away, fast. If things had gone different—if he was different—maybe he'd have a family like this now. A family of his own to love and look after and provide for. A wife who'd look at him—at over-tall, not-so-*schmaert* Jeremiah Weaver—like that, and a bright, cute little boy like Matthew to make them both smile.

Jeremiah shifted in his seat. The afternoon hadn't cooled off much, and it was hot riding in the buggy. He was sweaty and dirty, and his muscles ached from a long day of fencing. For most of the afternoon, he'd been looking forward to sitting down in a comfortable chair, maybe having something cool to drink.

He'd worked hard today, and he was tired. But—he glanced over at Anna. If he had a family like this and they were all going home together to a farm that belonged to them? He'd work five times as hard for such a life. Whatever it took, he'd do it, and he'd count it well worth the trouble.

His cheeks burned, and he turned his eyes hastily back to the road. He'd no business thinking such thoughts about Anna Speicher. He wasn't the sort of man she'd look at twice, so there was no point thinking any thoughts about her at all.

She was a sweet woman, a hard worker and smart as a whip. A real good mother, too. But likely she'd prefer a man who sat in the living room and read until bedtime, who was quick-witted and clever with his words. Who did work with his mind and not with his muscles.

She'd like a fellow like Jonah Miller, the one Barbara had ended up marrying after their wedding had been called off. Not that he begrudged Barbara her happiness. She'd hurt him, but that wasn't really her fault.

Gott made folks different, and He passed out blessings as He saw fit. Jeremiah accepted that, and he trusted the Lord's wisdom. As his *mamm* used to say, give thanks for the biscuit in your hand, and don't worry about what other folks are eating. He was very grateful for his blessings, and he tried not to think too much about the ones he was missing out on.

It was just that sometimes he felt an empty ache in his middle, as if something—or someone—was missing. He felt that way now.

But Matthew's happy chatter made the ride back to the farm go fast, and soon, Jeremiah was pulling the buggy to a stop by the store building. "I'll get this stuff unloaded," he offered gruffly. "Just tell me where you want things set."

"I help!" Matthew announced, and his mother shook her head.

"Best you stay out of Jeremiah's way."

The little boy looked crestfallen, and Jeremiah cleared his throat.

"There's some small things," he murmured. "If you don't mind him carrying them. I'll be careful to give him what can't be broken."

"That's nice of you, but he'll slow you down. I'm sure you've work of your own to see to, and we've already taken up so much of your time."

"It's all right." Jeremiah smiled down at Matthew, and a crumb-speckled face grinned back up at him. "A wise man never turns down good help."

Matthew did slow him down, but Jeremiah didn't mind. The two of them got the buggy unloaded as Anna whisked around her store, setting the boxes near whatever shelves she wanted them on. Since the paint was still sticky, filling the shelves would be a job for another day.

She seemed so happy that Jeremiah was almost sorry when he thumped the last box on the floor.

"That's it."

"All done!" Matthew echoed proudly, clunking down the little bag that Jeremiah had handed him. Jeremiah smiled and tousled his hair.

"Denki," he said solemnly. "You've done a real *gut* job."

The little boy beamed up at him, and the empty spot in Jeremiah's middle ached again. He cleared his throat.

"I think I've done all I can do, too, for now," Anna said. "I'll come back tomorrow and start putting everything in its place. I'll start making some flyers, too, to post around town. Hopefully I can be open for business in just a few more days."

"If you're done for today, I'll hitch up your horse," Jeremiah said.

He was halfway out the door, when Anna called his name.

He turned. *"Ja?"*

"I really appreciate your help. I know we're taking you from your own work, and that you've plenty of it to do. It wasn't my plan to ask you to haul all this over here this afternoon. Susie shouldn't have pushed you like she did, and then you had a little helper slowing you down, too."

"That's all right. I enjoyed it," Jeremiah assured her. "I don't get to spend much time with little ones. Your son's a fine boy."

Anna smiled. "Thank you for being so kind to him. You've a way with children." She paused before adding, "I'm surprised you don't have *kinder* of your own already."

There were questions hidden behind that remark—he heard it plain as plain. *Why?* she was asking. *Why don't you have yourself a nice family, Jeremiah Weaver, like every other able-bodied Amish man your age? What's wrong with you?*

Those weren't questions he planned to answer.

"Sorry, but I can't stand here talking. Like you said, I have my own work waiting, and the afternoon's fading fast.

I'll hitch up your horse, then I'll have to get back to fenc-ing. *Mach's gut*, Anna. Matthew."

He was out the door before she could reply. He strode toward the pasture, trying to forget the surprised and stricken look that had flashed across Anna's face.

He'd only told her the truth, he assured himself as he headed out to collect her mare from the pasture and get the buggy hitched. He'd his own work to do. Work he'd hoped for and prayed for, work he enjoyed.

The rest of it was true, too. The afternoon really had faded fast. Suddenly, all its sweet brightness was gone.

Chapter Seven

The following Saturday afternoon, Anna crouched on the floor of her old bedroom, wiping the baseboards with a cleaning rag. Church would be held in Elizabeth and Levi's home in two weeks, and the whole family had come together to help get ready. The men were outside clearing out the biggest barn where the service would be held, while the women scrubbed the house, getting into every crack and crevice.

It wasn't the first time Anna had helped prepare this house for church. Families took turns hosting services, so she'd gone through this ritual countless times during her growing-up years. It was a lot of work, and it never seemed to fall at a convenient time, but she'd always found it satisfying. The house sparkled and smelled so fresh afterward, and there was a sense of common purpose that she loved.

This year, though, was a little different.

"But why clean the bedroom floors now?" Mamm's tone fell just on the kinder side of impatient—as it had been most of the day. "It makes no sense, Elizabeth. You clean from the top to the bottom, which means you do the floors and the baseboards last. We've not even touched the living room and the kitchen yet, and those are what most people will see."

"I know that's the way you liked to do it, Mamm." Elizabeth, who was busy on the far side of the bedroom, sat back on her heels and rubbed her perspiring forehead with one sleeve. "That's a fine system, and it served you well. But I thought I'd try doing a full clean of the rooms that the family doesn't track through so much. Then I'll finish off the busier rooms just before Sunday."

"Well, I've never heard of such. But I suppose since you're in charge now..." Mamm looked as if she wanted to say something else, but she stayed silent.

Both Elizabeth and Mamm were trying hard to make this work, but the tension in the air was getting thicker by the minute.

"The flower beds and borders need weeding yet," Anna said. "That might be a good job to get out of the way." Elizabeth shot her a grateful look. Their mother had always loved fussing over the flowers and shrubs around the house.

"That's so." Mamm perked up. "They need trimming back, too. You should make the children work in the yard every day, Elizabeth," she said. "So it doesn't get ahead of you. I'll go out and see to that."

"*Denki*, Mamm. That would be wonderful," Elizabeth said.

"*Ja*, and I'd best get it done now, because I expect we'll have a lot extra to do at the last minute." With that gloomy pronouncement, Mamm headed outside. Elizabeth gave a short sigh as the back door thumped shut behind her.

Anna offered her sister a sympathetic smile. "It's hard," she said. "Mamm's been in charge here for such a long time. It's a big change for her to let you run things."

"I know. It's difficult for both of us. I don't want to be disrespectful, and mostly Mamm's ways work real well. But the responsibility of the house is mine now, and Levi says I have to take charge of it. But I understand it's not always easy for Mamm to see someone else managing her kitchen and all. Well," she went on, a different tone in her voice, "I expect you know something about that yourself."

Anna had turned her attention back to the baseboards. "This doesn't even seem like my room anymore, so it doesn't bother me. I got used to living away after Henry and I married, I guess, so it's not such a change for me."

"I wasn't talking about your old bedroom here. I meant over at the farm, now that you've rented out your and Henry's house—and to a bachelor, no less. Have you been inside the house? I mean, since he moved in?"

"Only the kitchen. It was a bit messy, but he's working hard right now to get his summer crops planted. I expect he's little time for cleaning."

"Too bad he's not married." Elizabeth finished cleaning her section. She rose and stretched her back before moving to the next wall. "A big house like that needs a woman to take care of it. But maybe he'll find himself a wife soon. I hear Trudy Schwartz is interested."

"In him and in every other bachelor in Hickory Springs." Mamm had poked her head back into the room. "The weeding trowel's not in its place on the back porch, Elizabeth. Did one of the children take it to play with?"

"I moved the garden supplies into the shed," Elizabeth said. "I'll show you where they are."

As the two women headed for the door, Mamm went on, "Trudy's almost thirty, and if she doesn't get married soon, she may not get married at all. It doesn't do to wait too long for such things." She threw a meaningful look over her shoulder at Anna. "Of course, from what I hear of this Jeremiah, Trudy might be better off looking elsewhere."

"Why would you say such a thing, Mamm?" Anna asked sharply. Her mother and sister looked at her with surprise. "It just… It seems very unkind."

"When I found out a stranger wanted to rent your farm, I did some asking about. Just to make sure he was of good character. You never know. Nobody I spoke to felt you'd lose anything by renting the place to him. He's trustworthy—at least as far as business dealings go."

Elizabeth looked intrigued. "What else did they say?"

"I don't want to gossip," her mother said—and then proceeded to do exactly that. "But, he was all set to marry a girl over in Owl Hollow, and the wedding was canceled at the very last minute."

"Oh!" Elizabeth looked at Anna. "Did you know that?"

"Susie mentioned it," Anna said shortly. Trudy had, too. When it came to Jeremiah, it seemed that canceled wedding was all anybody could talk about.

"Did she tell you why the wedding was called off?" her sister asked.

"Nee." Anna recalled how Jeremiah had cut off their conversation when she'd made that remark about him not having children. It served her right. She shouldn't have been fishing for information. "It's none of my business anyhow. As Mamm said, Jeremiah's honest and a good worker, and so long as he pays his rent, that's all that concerns me."

"Best that you keep it so." Mamm shook her head sadly. "From what I heard, the Esh family had nearly taken him to raise, so they were real hurt when he broke things off only a couple of days before the wedding. At least it sounds like their girl ended up all right. They say she made a match with a hardworking fellow who's likely to be a much better provider."

Anna almost laughed, remembering how doggedly Jeremiah was working in those hot fields. "Well, I don't know why the wedding didn't happen, but it couldn't be because Jeremiah's lazy. I've never seen anybody work harder."

"That may be so," her mother said. "But nowadays there's more to providing for a family than just muscle-work. According to what the girl's family says, this Jeremiah can't even read. In my day, that didn't matter so much. Any man willing to work hard could earn a decent living." She sighed. "It's different now. So many rules and forms to fill out. Amos Beiler's dairy was shut down just because he didn't fill out a paper right. Today a man has to be book-*schmaert* just to get by."

"I don't believe that. Jeremiah's plenty *schmaert*," Anna said. "And he can certainly read. Likely that family was just upset when the wedding was called off, and so they said things they shouldn't. Things that shouldn't be repeated."

She gave the baseboard a vicious wipe and then lifted her head to find her mother and Elizabeth exchanging a long look.

Her sister cleared her throat. "Let's go, Mamm, I'll show you where the trowel is."

"*Nee*, let your sister come with me. Between the two of us, we'll find what I need. Come along, Anna."

Anna rose, dusted her hands and followed her mother outside into the June sunshine. No doubt Mamm had something she wanted to say—likely something not so pleasant. Often in the past, this had been her mother's way of giving one of her children a private talking-to, asking them to come along on some errand or another.

Her mother didn't speak until they reached the shed. Sure enough, Elizabeth's gardening tools were neatly hung on the unpainted walls, so nicely organized that even Mamm could find no fault in it.

Anna took down the little three-pronged trowel and held it out to her mother, who accepted the tool absently. Her brow was furrowed, and Anna knew she was trying to find the best way to say what she wanted to say.

"You should be careful, Anna," her *mamm* said. "I'm not sure it's a *gut* thing…you spending so much time in this Jeremiah's company. In fact, I spoke to Charley about it the last time I saw him."

Anna frowned. Her mother had spoken to the bishop? "I'm not spending time with him, just on the farm. The store will be open when he's busy in the fields, and people will be coming and going. Jeremiah and I probably won't see each other very much at all." She braced herself. "What did Charley say?"

Charley wasn't terribly fussy as bishops went, but you never knew.

"He didn't see a problem with it," her mother admitted. "He said he'd had some concerns himself, to start with, and he'd asked some questions. But in the end, he decided it would be all right."

That was a relief. "If you're worried about Jeremiah's character, you needn't be. He's a nice fellow, helpful and good-hearted. And I'm sure he can read just fine. People shouldn't be going around saying such things. I think—"

"You've plenty of thoughts, *ja*," her mother interrupted. "That's what I wanted to speak to you about. You're real quick to defend a fellow you hardly know. I also see how fast he jumps to make you shelves and such, the minute he hears you need them. I know when a man and a woman are taking special notice of each other. So I'll say it again. You'd best be careful with this Jeremiah. Don't let your feelings run away with you."

"Oh." Anna didn't know what to say to that. She felt like a *youngie* again, being scolded for not behaving correctly.

"Now, don't get me wrong," Mamm continued. "I wish

Jeremiah nothing but *gut*, and I hope he does well with the farm. And I'd like to see you married again, you know that. You're getting so strong-minded, wanting to run your own business when you could have your pick of so many decent men and settle down again as a happy wife and mother. Ordinarily I'd be pleased to see you finally taking interest in a fellow."

"I'm not taking an interest."

"So you've said. But I can't help but notice, you're not near so strong-minded when it comes to this Jeremiah. You were determined to sell the farm, and now he's talked you into a whole different plan. Just think carefully before he talks you into anything else. Things are harder now than they used to be, and a lot of men—*schmaert* men—are struggling to provide for their families. A fellow who can't read? I just don't see how he could manage. Besides," she went on, "I'm not so sure of his character as you seem to be. There's something fishy about the explanation of why that wedding was canceled. But no matter the reason, it was wrong of him to wait until the last minute. It doesn't speak well of him, treating that girl and her family so poorly after their kindness to him. There, I've said my piece. You'd better get on back in the house. Elizabeth needs plenty of help if she's going to get this place ready for church—especially since she seems determined to do everything backward and upside down."

Her mother's tone made it clear that she considered the conversation over. Anna turned without speaking and walked back to the house. Probably a *gut* thing she held her tongue, because arguing with her mother wasn't a very respectful thing to do.

But Mamm really shouldn't be listening to such silly gossip. There was nothing wrong with Jeremiah's character, and he could read as well as anybody. Anna was sure of that.

Well. Almost sure.

She recalled how he'd refused to look at the terms she'd written out. And hadn't there been something about the cleaning products when she'd asked him to check to see what was in the buckets? He'd sidestepped that, too.

Anna frowned. Maybe there was something to this gossip, after all. If it was true, she felt sorry for him. It would be difficult for any person to go through life not being able to read. If she knew for certain, maybe she could find some way to help.

In any case, it shouldn't be very hard to find out.

Jeremiah stopped working on the fence long enough to swipe his forehead with his sleeve. He squinted up at the sky. Only a few clouds so far, but the breeze smelled like rain. Likely it would arrive before sunset, and that was good. His field needed it.

He'd learned to tell the weather working on the Esh farm. Samuel might not have been the best father in the world, nor the most loyal friend, but there was no doubt he was a skilled farmer. Jeremiah was thankful for all he'd learned from him.

He'd been thinking about that part of his life—his time choring for Samuel—a good bit since Anna had brought up his lack of a family. He shouldn't have been so short with her. She'd no way of knowing what a sore subject that was.

Jeremiah's *daed* had died young, leaving his wife and son to manage the best they could. They'd relied heavily on the church for support—and sadly, they weren't the first nor the last Weavers to do that. Weavers had a reputation for being lazy, an uncommon trait in their Amish community—and one very much frowned upon.

The church was always generous with struggling families, but Plain folks also believed that those who were able to work hard should do so. Jeremiah had started working for his neighbors at the age of nine, bringing in a few dollars here and there as best he could. After he'd finished his schooling, Samuel Esh had offered him a full-time job at his dairy, paying him partly with cash and partly with fresh milk, cheese and produce, Jeremiah couldn't say yes fast enough.

The arrangement had worked out fine for years. Until Samuel started hinting broadly to Jeremiah that his youngest daughter had special feelings for him.

He should have known better. But he didn't know so much about girls, and Barbara had always been shy and quiet. He just wished she could have found the courage to tell him the truth when he'd asked for that first buggy ride.

Things would sure have been simpler if she had.

But what happened was as much his fault as hers. He'd liked Barbara fine, but looking back now he realized what he'd really liked was the idea of being a part of the Esh family. Of one day inheriting the dairy farm—something else Samuel dropped plenty of hints about.

Wishful thinking. That's what that had been. As it turned out, Samuel had been doing a lot of that, too—or so Jeremiah learned just before the wedding, the day he'd found Barbara crying.

He felt guilty about what happened after. Not for canceling the wedding. He couldn't have done any different, not once he understood how Barbara really felt. But he hated to think about all that work and money wasted.

He also felt bad about the story he'd told Samuel. He'd not lied, but he'd sidestepped the truth a little, and that wasn't something he made a habit of. On the other hand, his shoulders were a lot broader than Barbara's and better able to bear the weight of her father's disappointment.

That weight had fallen fast and hard. Not a pleasant time to remember.

Jeremiah gazed across the field he'd painstakingly planted, smiling at the little bumps in the earth that meant his seeds were pushing up into the light. As hard and as embarrassing as all that trouble had been, it had led him to where he stood today—on a farm that might one day be his very own, earned by the sweat of his own brow.

Gott had brought *gut* out of the bad, just as He promised to do, and Jeremiah was thankful for it.

"Jeremiah?"

He glanced over his shoulder. Anna was walking across the yard, Matthew trailing behind her. She carried a large cup in one hand.

"Woof?" Sunny wagged her tail hopefully. She'd been camped out beside him most of the day, watching his work from whatever shady spot was handy with occasional visits to the water bowl he'd set out for her. She was bored and ready for company.

"Go on, then," he said with a chuckle. The little dog jumped up and scampered toward Matthew, barking delightedly. She danced around the boy, making him squeal with laughter. Anna smiled down at them for a minute before heading over to Jeremiah.

As she got closer, Jeremiah did another quick test sniff. This time it wasn't the weather he was checking—but himself. He was sweaty, and this shirt needed washing pretty badly. Hopefully Anna would stay downwind.

"I brought you something cool to drink." Anna held out the cup, which turned out to be brimful of lemonade. "It's a hot day to be working in the sun. A man could get sick if he doesn't drink enough. You should probably fill a thermos with cold water in the morning and take it to the fields with you."

"I did." He accepted the cup and nodded toward the chubby jug he'd stashed in a shady spot. "I'm used to looking after myself. But—" he added hastily "—it's nice of you to bring me a drink. You shouldn't have taken the trouble."

He suspected he knew why she had. The lemonade was her way of making amends for stepping wrong with him the other day, but the small kindness had the opposite effect than she'd intended. Now he felt even worse about being so short with her.

"I didn't mind," Anna was saying. "I've been cooped up in the store all day, opening boxes and getting things organized."

"That's a job." Jeremiah had unloaded his share of boxes, bags and barrels. Stocking storerooms and shelves took time and energy.

Anna didn't look much the worse for wear, though. Her face was rosy, and there was a happy light in her eyes. Storekeeping suited her. Not surprising, he supposed, seeing as how she'd grown up with a storekeeper for a *daed*. He must have been a real *schmaert* fellow, and good with his books. Anna took after him.

"I wondered if you might be willing to come up for a minute, once you're done out here for the day? There are a few things too heavy for me to move. Not much," she added quickly. "Just a couple of things. If you don't mind."

"I don't mind."

"Denki." A quick, heart-stopping flash of a smile. She reached out to touch the roll of wire with one finger. "The fence is looking good. Nice and strong."

"It'll do, I think." Fencing was another thing he'd learned from Samuel. Dairy cows liked to test wires, and they always thought the grass on the other side of the pasture fence looked the greenest.

"Could I ask you a question, Jeremiah?"

She sounded *naerfich*, although he couldn't imagine why. "Sure."

"What was wrong with this other fence? The one that was already here? Couldn't you fix it? Why put up a second one so close? That's a lot of material, and a lot of expense. And isn't this going to be a vegetable garden?"

He took a swallow of lemonade before he answered. "*Ja*, it is. Beans, corn and peas, things the local markets are wanting."

Another flicker of a smile, as sweet as the lemonade she'd made. "Well, the vegetables aren't likely to escape, are they? Why do you need two fences to keep them in?"

"It's not what I'm keeping in. It's what I'm keeping out. Deer," he added when she looked at him, puzzled. "I'll have no crops at all if I can't keep the deer out. For big farms, it doesn't matter so much, but I've only the time and the money to plant a few acres, and I'm going to need every vegetable I can get. I can't afford to share with the deer."

"Oh." Her face fell, and she nibbled thoughtfully on her bottom lip. Behind her, Matthew and Sunny had tired of their running and jumping game and had tumbled into a heap on the grass under a shade tree. Both of them were panting. "But—" Anna started, then stopped.

"What?"

"It's just…maybe you don't know, but deer…" She looked up at him, the brow under her white *kapp* puckered with worry. "Deer can jump really high."

He'd taken another drink from the cup just as she spoke,

and the mixture of amusement and surprise he felt made him choke. He spluttered for a few minutes, coughing up the lemonade he'd inhaled.

"I'm so sorry," Anna said seriously. "I should have come out here before and told you."

"Told me." He coughed one last time and wiped his mouth. "About the deer."

"*Ja.* They'll jump this fence in no time. They could jump one twice as high."

Jeremiah paused, wondering how to phrase this gently. He'd been made to feel *dumm* more than once himself, and he didn't like making other people feel that way.

"Anna, I've never owned a farm before, but I worked on one for nine years. I know about deer, and I know how to keep them out of gardens. Deer can jump high. You're right about that. What they can't do is jump high and long at the same time."

Her face had shifted from worried to puzzled. "I don't understand."

"One fence this height won't keep out the deer. But two, set just a few feet apart will. They don't like jumping down in tight spaces, and they can't jump both fences. That's why I'm fencing it in double. It's an expense, but it's also an investment."

"Oh!" She looked over the doubled fence line. "I see. You're right, I think. I've seen a deer stand almost on its hind legs to go over a fence. But I don't think they'd be able to go up and over at the same time."

"*Nee*, they can't. I tried it out on the farm where I was before. It worked real well."

"That was *schmaert*." Anna sounded delighted, as if his discovery pleased her. "I don't know anybody else in Hickory Springs who does that."

"It's not practical for bigger fields. But for one this size, it works out."

The admiration in her eyes was doing funny things to his insides. He took his time finishing off the lemonade so he wouldn't be expected to talk. He struggled to squelch the pride he felt rising up in his chest. It was a *gut* thing nobody had ever admired him much before. He'd have ended up with a puffed-up sense of himself and plenty to confess to the church if they had.

"Well." Anna glanced behind her. Matthew and Sunny were leaning against the trunk of a tree, the dog snuggled against the boy's chest, both of them looking as contented as could be. "Let me know when you have a few minutes to move those things for me. Now we'd better let you get back to your work."

He'd plenty of it to do, and he'd already learned that the days weren't near long enough to get everything in. But he heard himself saying, "I'll come on up and move the stuff for you now. I'm ready for a break anyhow."

They walked together across the pasture, Matthew and Sunny running ahead. Anna smiled as she watched them. Jeremiah knew because his eyes kept returning to her face, in spite of his efforts to keep them focused somewhere—anywhere—else.

Anybody—well, any fellow—would have the same problem, he told himself. *Ach*, but Anna was a pretty one. There was a special sweetness in the curve of her cheek and in the gentle way her eyes rested on the little one and the pup. This woman had known her share of hardship and sorrow. In fact, she'd had more of those things earlier than most women did, but her grief hadn't made her bitter. Only kinder and stronger.

He admired that. Those folks who wondered why Gott allowed hard things to come into people's lives might take a look at Anna's Speicher's face—to see the beauty that trouble could bring out in a person.

A breeze stirred, ruffling her dress and bringing the nice, clean scent of soap to his nose. Anna laughed.

"It's nice," she said. "How the wind moves over the pastures here. We always had a pleasant breeze when we sat on the porch of an evening."

"*Ja,* it's real nice," Jeremiah said. "Do you ever miss it? The farm?"

He'd been wondering about that. It was hard for him to believe that anyone could leave this farm, and never miss it. It was a beautiful place.

"*Nee,*" Anna said quickly. Then her expression shifted, and she looked thoughtful for a moment. "Well, there are some things I miss. Living closer to town is different. More traffic, and such, so I worry about Matthew playing outside. And then, of course, living with Susie—" She broke off, shooting him an apologetic look.

She needn't have felt uncomfortable. He knew what that was like, living under someone else's roof. "That would be hard, I reckon. Living in another woman's house when you're used to having your own."

"Susie is very pleasant," Anna said carefully. "I couldn't ask for a better situation. But, of course, it's a little difficult, especially with a child."

"I can see that. I've lived in rented rooms. That's one of the things I like best about being here. Having the whole place to myself."

"But you don't have it all to yourself, not anymore. I'm here most days now. Pestering you to build shelves and move heavy things."

"I don't mind. Fellow my size gets used to helping with such things. It's never bothered me."

They'd reached the yard, and Matthew was stopped by the latch on the wooden gate. Jeremiah stepped forward and flipped it for him.

The child looked up at him and smiled sweetly. For a second he looked so much like his *mamm* that it was startling. "*Denki*, big man." He ran through the gate, Sunny dancing at his heels.

"His name is Jeremiah," Anna called after her son. "I'm sorry," she said. "I'll speak to him again."

He laughed. "Like I said, I'm used to it."

"Have you always...you know...been—" She stuttered to an uncomfortable stop.

"Oversized? Pretty much. Since I can remember, anyhow. I was always head and shoulders above most other fellows. Never bothered me much. Comes in handy, more often than not."

Anna considered that. "I guess it would, *ja*." They'd reached the store building, and she pushed open the door. "You and the *hund* can play here," she told Matthew. "Just outside the door so Mamm can see you." She waited for her child's nod before leading the way inside.

Jeremiah ducked inside the door and looked around, impressed by the change he saw. This was a far cry from the junk-littered building where he'd found Sunny.

Shelves lined the clean, white walls, crowded now with neat lines of jars, bottles and cans. She'd brought in a small table and had created a pretty arrangement of homemade jams and jellies, and even some jars of local honey. The far wall had large canning jars filled with spices, each bearing a neat, handwritten label. Small paper sacks were stacked nearby, ready for customers to fill with whatever amount they needed.

The scent of fresh paint mingled pleasantly with the

smell of the spices. Blue curtains were drawn to the side over the windows, which were halfway open to allow the breeze in. A chalkboard was angled in front of the counter he'd made, covered with neat handwriting.

"What do you think?" Anna asked.

She was watching him, twisting her fingers in front of her apron. She looked *naerfich* again, which surprised him. There was no reason she should care what his opinion was.

"It's hard to believe this is the same building."

"Most of that goes to your credit." She was smiling, but she still seemed uneasy. "Do the prices I've set seem fair?" She nodded toward the chalkboard.

Jeremiah glanced at the writing, words and numbers, neatly lined up. He could puzzle them out if he had to—he recognized a couple of the words right off. But the rest would take him too long, and Anna was watching him awful close. He felt the familiar squeeze in his chest that always came along with being asked to read in front of someone.

"I don't know much about pricing," he said. "But I'll tell you this." He walked over to examine the chalkboard more closely. "I can mount this for you. On the front of the counter maybe. Otherwise, it's likely to fall over. The wall would have been a better spot, but since you've shelves on all of those—"

"*Ja*, that's true." She looked disappointed, but she shrugged. "There's not much room in here. It would be nice if you'd nail it to the front of the cabinet. If it's not too much trouble, I mean."

"No trouble. But we'll not nail it. We'll put some nails into the counter itself and some metal loops on the back of the board so you can take it off and on. Otherwise, you'd have to crouch down any time you want to change a price. You'll likely get tired of that."

"That's a *schmaert* idea." Funny how his simple suggestion

had perked her right up. And—more importantly—distracted her from her question about the prices.

"And as for the storage, if you need more than you've got here, you're more than welcome to store things in the house."

"Nee." Anna shook her head. "I couldn't—"

"It would be no bother to me. I'm just one man, so I rattle around that house like a bean in a coffee can. There's plenty of room for you to store your extras down in the cellar."

"It would make things simpler," she admitted. "That's kind of you, Jeremiah. *Denki.*"

"You're welcome. But don't try to carry anything heavy down to the cellar yourself. Just let me know what you want and where to put it."

"You're being very kind," Anna repeated, but her brow was furrowed. "Jeremiah—"

"Vass?"

"Jeremiah, I wanted to ask—" She hesitated, then said in a rush, "What do you think about those quilt pieces?"

He was almost sure that wasn't what she'd started out to say, and he knew less about quilts than he did about prices. But he looked in the direction she pointed.

She'd tacked small, quilted pieces on the backs of the taller shelves, where they would show above the tops of the jars. She'd also made use of any empty space between the shelves to display the fabric pieces.

They were pretty enough, lots of nice, bold colors, although he'd no idea what anybody would use them for. But then again, Englischers often wanted all sorts of things he saw no point in, so likely these would sell well.

"I like 'em," he said, since she seemed to be waiting for his answer. "They add a nice bit of brightness to the room." Although, in his private opinion, any room Anna Speicher was standing in was plenty bright already.

"Can you guess who made them?" Before he could answer, she hurried on. "Look at one of the tags and see!"

There went that squeeze in his chest again. No need, he told himself. This was an easy one. "I know without looking. Lilah Miller made 'em." The storekeeper's new wife was skilled with her needle and favored bold colors like the ones here. He'd seen her work before.

That disappointed look was on Anna's face again. "*Ja*, Lilah made them for me. And she was doing me a favor, since she mostly sells her quilts at Eben's store."

Jeremiah nodded. "Lilah's a good-hearted woman. Her tongue can be a bit sharp, but she means nothing by it."

"Each one shows a different quilting pattern." Anna walked over to one made of red and white triangles. "Can you guess what this one's called?"

"*Nee*, I'd not have a clue."

"Come see," Anna invited, wiggling the little white tag.

Suspicion prickled across Jeremiah's shoulders. "I'd best be getting back to my fencing," he said. "So if you'll show me what you want moved…"

Anna dropped the little tag, but she didn't answer him right away. Instead she studied him, her brow creased, her hands clenched in front of her apron.

Jeremiah's neck prickled again. Whatever she was about to say, he was pretty sure he wasn't going to like it.

He was also pretty sure he knew what it would be. He hoped he was wrong, that he'd managed to sidestep her guesses, but from that look on her face—

Before he could finish the thought, Anna took a deep breath, like somebody about to dive into deep water.

"Jeremiah? I don't mean to be unkind, but… Can't you read?"

Chapter Eight

Jeremiah went still, a dark flush creeping up to stain his neck and cheeks. Anna's heart sank. She'd embarrassed him.

"I'm sorry," she said hurriedly. "I shouldn't have asked."

He swallowed. "That's all right. Do you really need anything moved? Or did you just want to…" He trailed off.

"Oh! Well—" She flushed. "It's nothing that can't wait, I guess."

"In that case, like I said, I'd better get back to work. I have a lot of fencing to finish."

"Of course," she said miserably.

Without another word, he walked out of the door. For an instant as he crossed over the threshold, his broad shoulders blocked the sunlight, dimming the little store. Then he was gone.

But the dimness lingered throughout the afternoon, as Anna busied herself adding finishing touches to her store. She was planning to open in a week, and she had more signs to letter out, but her heart wasn't in it. She kept remembering the flicker of pain in Jeremiah's eyes.

She'd not meant to hurt him. She'd only wanted so badly to prove that what people were saying about him was wrong. She'd wanted to be able to triumphantly assure her mother—and anybody else saying such things—that Jeremiah Weaver could read just fine.

Instead, it seemed she'd proved their point. He'd dodged her invitations to read the simple words on the chalkboard and the tags on Lilah's quilt squares just as he'd dodged reading other things in the past.

But none of that mattered now.

She finished rearranging jars of bulk spices on a shelf and stepped back to check it. But instead of looking at the spices, she found herself admiring the shelves themselves—so neat and so sturdy, and perfectly fitted around the windows. Anchored down safely, too, so she didn't have to worry about them falling over.

She glanced out the door where her son was playing happily with Sunny. The dog had stayed behind after Jeremiah left. She was pouncing playfully at the toddler, then jumping back. She sure didn't resemble the frightened, skinny animal who'd left muddy tracks across her living room floor. This dog was healthy, bright-eyed and happy.

Thanks to Jeremiah's kindness.

Anna trailed one hand across the smooth surface of the counter he'd built. Just the right size, and so nice-looking, too. He'd even built some storage on its hidden side, which was real thoughtful of him.

And how had she thanked him? By poking at what must be a very sore spot. She should have minded her own business.

A buggy rolled up beside the store, and a second later, Susie Raber rounded the corner of the building. She paused long enough in the yard to give Matthew and the dog each a sugar cookie, then she hurried inside, looking as energetic and cheerful as always.

"Oh, my, Anna!" Susie stopped three steps in and looked

around the room admiringly. "Isn't this something? It looks wonderful! People will flock to this place, once they hear of it. Speaking of that, do you have your grand opening flyer ready for me to tape up in the bakery window?"

"I do. *Denki*, Susie!" Anna tried her best to sound happy, but she must not have managed too well. Her friend studied her with a concerned expression.

"What's wrong?"

"Nothing," Anna assured her quickly. "At least, nothing with the store. But I'm afraid I've caused a problem with Jeremiah."

"Oh?" Susie tsked her tongue. "I'm sure it's nothing that can't be remedied. Why don't you tell me about it, and let's see if I can help."

Although she was embarrassed to admit how unfeeling she'd been, Anna recounted what had happened as honestly as she could. Susie's expression never changed. She only looked thoughtful—although she glanced up sharply when Anna explained how she'd wanted to boost Jeremiah's reputation.

"You know," Susie said when Anna had finished. "I've wondered a bit. He covers it well, so I was never sure, even though he'd been delivering to the bakery for years. But now and again, I noticed things, even though he almost never made a mistake."

"Imagine," Anna said softly, shaking her head. "How hard that would be for him. He must listen real close to everything that's said and have a sharp memory to be able to get by so well."

"I'd think so, *ja*." That funny little smile tilted up the corners of Susie's mouth again. "I had a friend once who was near blind, and I was always amazed by what she could do. She was a better knitter than any of the rest of us, even with her eyesight problems. She joked that she'd learned to see through her fingers. She just paid better attention, I think."

Anna considered this. *Ja*, Jeremiah paid attention, too. Like noticing that she'd need those shelves before anybody had thought of asking him to make some. "I shouldn't have said anything."

"Probably not," Susie conceded. "But I don't think Jeremiah's one to hold a grudge. Here." She set a plump white paper bag on the counter. "Take him some sugar cookies. In my experience, men are a lot more forgiving when goodies are involved. Especially bachelors."

"That's not a bad idea. Maybe I'll walk over and have a word with him before Matthew and I leave for the day."

"It's hard to talk seriously with a little one around. Why don't I take Matthew with me? He can help me put up the sign, and then we'll go on home. That way you and Jeremiah can talk as long as you like."

Anna shot a suspicious glance at her friend, but Susie's face was blandly innocent. And it would be easier to talk about such things without Matthew underfoot. He was an obedient child, mostly, but he did tend to get a little fussy as the afternoon wore on, and he was bound to be tired after playing so hard with Sunny today.

"All right," she decided. "*Denki*, Susie."

"Oh, I'm happy to do it." She did look happy. In fact, she was humming when she went outside to collect Matthew for the ride home.

Anna, however, wasn't very happy at all. She dreaded speaking to Jeremiah. What if Susie was wrong, and he wasn't ready to accept her apology yet? Or worse, what if she put her foot in her mouth a second time? She tried to plan out exactly how she'd ask his forgiveness, but everything she came up with sounded wrong.

She kept watch through the windows, and in the late afternoon, when she saw Jeremiah heading in from the field, she mustered up her courage, picked up the bag of cookies and walked out to meet him.

"Susie left you some treats," she said, holding out the bag.

"That was generous of her." Cookies or not, he didn't seem so pleased to see her. He also looked very tired—and when he wiped his dirty hands on his work pants before accepting the sack of cookies, he left a smear of blood on the material.

"You're bleeding!"

"*Ach*, well." Jeremiah inspected his hand and shrugged. "It's just a little cut. The wire's sharp, and these things happen, especially when you get in a hurry. The fencing's done. That's all that matters."

Apprehension tickled across Anna's shoulders. She'd heard Henry say the same thing dozens of times.

"It's not *all* that matters," she told him. "You matter, too. You need to take care of yourself, Jeremiah. An infected cut will only slow down the work in the long run. Let me see your hand. I'll help you clean it up."

She held her own hand out in invitation, but Jeremiah shook his head stubbornly. "*Denki*, but I've looked after myself for a long time." His voice held a new, hard edge. "Myself and other folks, too, when I see someone who needs help. A fellow doesn't have to read so *gut* to be able to do that."

Saddened, Anna dropped her hand. "I know that. I certainly should, seeing as how I'm one of those you've been helping. I've upset you, and I'm so sorry, Jeremiah. I shouldn't have asked about the reading."

He looked away, over the sprouting fields, his usually friendly face set in hard lines. "It's nothing to do with you, that's all."

Anna wanted to argue, but she couldn't. He had a point. She was meddling where she shouldn't be.

"You're right," she admitted. "It's none of my business." Maybe she should have stopped there, but she didn't like this discord between them. "And neither is the fact that you're bleeding. I know. But please do be careful, Jeremiah, especially when you're tired. Farming's hard work, and it never seems to be done. If a fellow's not careful, he'll wear himself out, and that's when things worse than little cuts start to happen. Trust me, I know."

Jeremiah looked at her then, and his expression softened. "You think that's why your *mann* got hurt? Because he'd worked until he was worn out?"

Anna hesitated, surprised at the question. Nobody had ever asked her that before. People wanted to know what had happened after an accident, but nobody ever asked why. Such things weren't discussed after a death. You were expected to accept Gott's will, as best you could, and go on in faith.

"I think so, *ja*. Henry was very tired that week. Everything had gone wrong. The weather wasn't cooperating, and things were breaking right and left. He was worried and not sleeping so well and hurrying to catch up on his work. He must have forgotten to set the brake, and—" She stopped, pushing away the painful memory of that awful day. "But you're right in saying that it's not my place to ask nosy questions. So I'll just say, I hope you do well here, and I hope you'll be very careful, especially when you're tired. I would hate to see anybody else get hurt on this farm. *Mach's gut*." She turned to go.

She'd only taken four steps before Jeremiah's deep voice rumbled softly behind her.

"I can read."

She looked over her shoulder. His face was ruddy with embarrassment, but dogged determination shone in his dark eyes. A muscle twitched in his jaw as he studied his strong, dirty hands, holding the flimsy white bakery bag.

"I just read slower than most. Well." He looked up at her. "Slower than pretty much everybody," he amended.

Anna wasn't sure what to say. He looked so shamed, and she felt shamed herself that she'd thrown his problem in his face. Maybe she'd not meant to hurt him, but clearly she had.

"Nobody's good at everything," she said finally. "Gott makes us so, I think, so that we can learn to depend on Him and on each other." She offered a cautious smile. "Like I had to depend on you to make my shelves."

"I wish everybody saw it that way," Jeremiah muttered.

"Maybe I could help you," Anna offered tentatively. "With the reading. I'm no teacher, but I did all right in school. If you want, I could try."

"It would do no good. The problem's not a lack of teaching. It's something in here." He tapped the side of his head with one finger. "Something doesn't work like it should, not when it comes to reading. Other things, I do just fine."

He gazed over the fields. "I've missed farming," he said. "The work is hard, but it's work I can do and do well. I like the quiet and the elbow room, and not spending most of every day driving a wagon and working in storerooms. I like this farm, and I like this town, and I like—" He broke off, suddenly. He glanced at her, then away. "I want to stay here for good if I can."

Anna's stomach had a sudden case of the flutters, and she wasn't sure why. He'd said nothing out of the ordinary. "Then I'll pray you'll get to do that."

"Denki." Jeremiah shifted his weight from one boot to

another, and Sunny gave a worried whine. "You know, I was planning on being married once, back in Owl Hollow. I broke it off."

Anna felt as if they were treading into dangerous territory. "I'm sure you had your reasons."

"There were reasons," Jeremiah admitted slowly. "Not all of them were mine. Afterward, her family was upset about it, particularly her father. He knew about my trouble with reading. I'd worked for him long enough that I couldn't have kept it a secret. It never seemed to bother him much, and he never told anybody about it. But when Barbara and I called off the wedding, he said a few things to his friends." He shrugged. "I guess to let them know I wasn't any great loss, after all."

"Then that man should be ashamed of himself." That wasn't a nice thing to say, particularly about someone she'd never met, but just at the moment she didn't care. It was true.

"*Nee*, Samuel's not a bad man, and he'd been *gut* to me over the years. Closest thing to a *daed* I ever had. He was just embarrassed and upset because he'd wanted—" Jeremiah stopped and shook his head. "Anyhow, between that and the wedding trouble, folks didn't ever treat me quite the same. So, I'd appreciate it if you'd keep this to yourself. I'm not asking you to lie," he added quickly. "Just to not make a point of it. I want to make a strong beginning here in Hickory Springs, and I don't need people to start off doubting me."

Some of them already did, Anna thought, remembering her *mamm*'s warning. And she'd already spoken with Susie about it. But she wasn't going to mention that—Susie would keep the information to herself. "I won't say anything, of course. But they won't doubt you anyway, not once they get to know you."

"I hope you're right." He offered her a half smile. "Then again, I'd say the folks in Owl Hollow knew me pretty well, and it didn't seem to make much difference there. Now, I think we've got this settled between us, so we'd both best be getting about our business. *Mach's gut*, Anna. Tell Susie thanks for the cookies, and let me know when you're ready to get those things you mentioned moved. I'll get it done. Come along, then, Sunny." He whistled to his adoring dog and turned away, heading for the house.

Anna watched him go, biting down so hard on her bottom lip that it stung. So her *mamm* had been right—Jeremiah couldn't read too well. But somewhere along the way, he'd sure learned an awful lot about kindness—and forgiveness.

Surely that ought to count for something.

"Now, see that there? That's a weed." Jeremiah pointed to a bit of coffee weed poking up between the bean plants.

Matthew crouched and scrabbled in the dirt with chubby fingers. "Pull it up," he said, his face serious.

"That's right. We pull it up so the beans can grow big and strong." He leaned on his hoe, watching as Matthew tugged the little sprout out of the ground. The little boy held it up triumphantly.

"You made a good job of that," Jeremiah told him. "See? These are the roots. If you'd left them in the ground, the weed would have grown back. But you didn't, so now the weed is gone."

"Gone!" Matthew echoed happily. He rose and walked down the row, stepping dangerously close to the growing beans. Jeremiah reached out with his free hand to nudge the child back on the path.

As he knelt to help Matthew locate the next weed, Jeremiah breathed in the good smells of growing things, freshly turned earth—and a whiff of the manure pile he'd started behind the barn. He smiled.

Ja, he liked farming.

Of course, with little Matthew "helping," he wasn't getting much work done today. He probably ought to feel worse about that than he did. It was a good day for weeding. Last night's rain had softened up the dirt nicely, but the garden wasn't too wet to work in. And since the weeds loved the rich dirt and the moisture just as much as the vegetable plants did, there was plenty of work to do.

Alone, he'd have had half the plot done by now. As it was, he was still working on the first row.

"Not that one," he said for the dozenth time. "That's a bean plant. See the leaves? Kind of shaped like hearts, aren't they? Now, that grass right there?" He pointed. "You can pull that up."

"Weed!" Matthew squatted, sticking his little rump out and working to get a grip on the sprig of grass. "*Nee*, Sunny," he said, fussing at the dog who'd stepped up to sniff-check whatever her favorite child was getting into. "I do it myself. Gotta get woots," he added seriously.

The dog whuffed a resigned sigh and settled down in a soft patch of dirt, where she could keep an eye on Matthew. She loved Jeremiah, but she clearly had some concerns about him as a babysitter.

Given how dirty the boy was getting, Anna might agree with the dog, but Jeremiah was enjoying himself. Little boys washed clean easy enough, and he could always finish the weeding after Anna's grand opening day was over, and she and Matthew had gone home for the day.

He squinted back toward the store building. When he'd stopped by midmorning to wish her well on her big opening day, he'd noticed how flustered she was, trying to keep

Matthew busy and out of trouble. The store had been quiet, but he figured she'd see an uptick in her business once Plain folks got done with their morning work. And, of course, Englischers didn't usually get up very early, so likely they'd be along later, too.

She'd be busy then, so he'd volunteered to take Matthew out with him. He'd been a little surprised that Anna had accepted the offer so readily. Maybe it was only because Matthew had looked so happy at the idea of tagging along with Jeremiah, but she'd not hesitated even a moment.

"Susie's working and Mamm had a doctor's appointment today and couldn't keep him," she'd explained. "He'll be happier outside with you and Sunny, if you're sure he won't hinder your work."

"I'm in no hurry today," he'd assured her. Since then, he and the boy had been working their way through Jeremiah's list of chores. It was slow going, but Jeremiah didn't mind.

It was fun, this. Showing a little one about gardening and such. The boy was so happy and fascinated by everything, from grasshoppers to weeds.

"Dat bean." Matthew pointed to a tiny plant. "Right, big man?"

"That's right! Good eye. I see a weed, though. Do you?"

Matthew pointed to another sprig of grass.

"*Ja, gut.* Pull it up."

Matthew set to work. He was an obedient little boy— and a quick learner, too, for one so young. *Schmaert*—like his *mamm*.

And probably his *daed*, too, Jeremiah reminded himself. He'd not known Henry Speicher, but he'd had the *gut* sense to court Anna, hadn't he? Besides, she'd never have been interested in anyone who wasn't *schmaert*.

Jeremiah's happy mood dimmed. He squatted beside Matthew, who'd moved on to the next bit of grass.

It bothered him that Anna knew about his reading problems. It shouldn't. They'd settled things between themselves, and he trusted her not to spread the word around. So, what difference did it make? If anything, it was likelier to make things easier. He'd not have to do so much pretending now.

There was no reason for him to feel so ashamed about something he couldn't help. That sort of embarrassment was just the back side of pride, and the church had plenty to say about that.

He'd been reminding himself of that ever since their conversation, but so far he'd not felt much better. Well— he glanced down at his little companion—not until today, anyhow. Matthew had cheered him up pretty well.

He glanced toward the store building and frowned. There still weren't any buggies or cars parked alongside it, in spite of the big hand-lettered sign he'd helped Anna place by the road earlier today. So far her opening day seemed awful quiet.

That was a shame. She'd been so excited this morning. There'd been a happy sparkle in her eyes as she'd moved around her little store, tweaking things into place.

Well, he hoped she wasn't too discouraged. Business might pick up yet. There was still a while until closing time.

But when he and Matthew walked back to the store around six, the parking area was just as empty as it had been all day. Matthew went straight through the door and behind the counter, probably after the cookies he'd been chattering about for the last few minutes.

But Jeremiah hesitated at the doorway.

Anna was moving around the store again, straightening

various items, but with none of the happy energy she'd shown this morning. Her shoulders were slumped and there was a strained look around her mouth. However, she managed a smile when her son emerged from behind the counter, clutching two big cookies.

"One for me. One for Sunny," he explained.

"All right. Take them outside, so I don't have crumbs to sweep up." As Matthew trotted through the door, she turned back to Jeremiah. "*Denki* for watching him. I'm afraid I wasted your time, though. I've had only three customers the whole day long."

"It's only the first day. Sometimes it takes a while for a new business to take hold. I expect you ask anybody, they'd tell you the same. I wouldn't worry about it."

"I'm trying not to. It's just… I've sunk an awful lot of my money into buying the store goods. I guess I shouldn't have bought so much to start with. I felt so sure people would come. So many said they would, but…"

He felt a flare of irritation on Anna's behalf. Folks were like that, even the well-meaning ones. What they said they'd do and what they actually did were often two different things.

He tried to think of something encouraging to say.

"Oh, they may come yet. Maybe they forgot, or they had something else to do today. It's a busy season, summer. Wait and see. Business will pick up."

"I hope you're right." Anna slid a jar to the left and then back to the right. "If it doesn't, my *mamm* will have plenty to say."

"What will she say, then?"

Anna shrugged and kept her eyes down. "The same thing she's been saying. That I should forget about the idea of running a store and get married again instead."

Married again. Jeremiah's heart gave a heavy thump,

and he fought an urge to kick the doorpost. As pretty and sweet as Anna was, she'd have plenty of choices if word got out that she was considering remarriage. She'd be married before she knew what happened.

"Is that what you want, yourself? To marry again?" He forgot to breathe as he waited for her to answer.

It seemed a simple enough question to him. But Anna sure didn't seem to know how to answer it.

"Vass?" She stared at him, the cleaning rag dangling from her hand. "I—I don't know," she whispered finally.

She looked so stricken that Jeremiah was ashamed of himself. He had no business asking her such a personal question. He'd not liked it so much when she'd asked about his reading, had he?

"Ach, well," he said quickly. "Once the store gets going, you won't have to worry about it anyhow. You'll be able to support yourself just fine without a husband."

Anna blinked several times. "That's true." she said slowly. "I could stay single for the rest of my life if the store does all right."

He couldn't tell if she was happy about that idea or not. She just sounded…stunned.

"And it will," he assured her. "You can't let a bad first day discourage you."

"Nee." Anna put down the cleaning rag. *"Nee,* of course not." She walked over and collected a bag and a cooler from behind the counter. "I think I'd better go now, Jeremiah. It's been a long day, and I'm sure Matthew's tired. I…thank you for watching him today. I guess I'll see you tomorrow. Would you mind closing up when you leave?"

"Nee. But wait, and I'll help you hitch your—"

"That's all right. I can do it myself!" She called over her shoulder as she hurried out the door to collect her son.

Jeremiah started to follow her, then decided against it. He'd wait here, out of sight, until she was gone. Obviously, he'd made her uncomfortable, poking his nose in where it didn't belong. Whether or not Anna wanted to remarry was none of his business.

But he was privately glad she didn't plan on rushing into anything. At least, not so long as the store worked out.

He looked around at the shelves he'd built for her, still as well-stocked and neat as they had been this morning.

He glanced at a pile of leftover advertising flyers on the corner of the counter, and then back through the window at Anna, who was brushing dirt off Matthew's pants. Jeremiah had paused by the pump and washed about half the garden off the boy's face and hands, but there'd been little he could do about the clothes.

Swiftly, he picked up several of the flyers. Once Anna left, he'd hitch up Chock and take a drive to Owl Hollow. More tourists shopped there than in Hickory Springs, and he knew most of the shopkeepers from his old delivery route. They'd put up flyers if he asked them to.

He'd not say anything to Anna about it, though. He didn't want to get her hopes up.

But if this didn't bring in some shoppers, he'd see what else he could think of. He wanted this store to be a success.

Because if it wasn't, Anna might start listening to her *mamm*, and in Jeremiah's opinion, no woman ought to be pushed into marrying, not by a parent, nor anybody else.

Chapter Nine

Anna finished braiding her hair for the night and flipped the thick plait over her shoulder. Quietly she opened her bedroom door, walked a few steps down the hallway and pushed open the door next to her own.

Moonlight streamed through the window, falling over Matthew, who was sound asleep in his narrow bed, a stuffed rabbit tucked under one arm. The gentle breeze trickling through the window screen cooled the small room to a pleasant temperature and carried in the songs of crickets and frogs and the occasional sound of an Englischer's car on the highway.

Although it hadn't been part of their original agreement, Susie had suggested Anna use her extra bedroom for Matthew. The room was small, only big enough for the bed, a little wooden dresser and a basket for toys and books.

But it was comfortable and convenient, and since Susie was charging her no additional rent for it, it was a true blessing. Anna offered a silent prayer of gratitude to Gott, looking down at her son and trying to absorb the peacefulness of the room.

Peace had been in short supply today. The store opening hadn't gone so well, and afterward there had been that unsettling conversation with Jeremiah.

When he'd asked her whether she wanted to marry again, she'd fumbled over her answer, an answer she'd settled in her mind a good while back. And then, when he'd made that remark about the store, that if it did well, she'd not have to worry about marrying again, the truth had hit her—like a bolt of lightning out of the blue.

She didn't want to be single for the rest of her life. Someday—not right now, of course—but someday not so far off, she'd like to be married again.

She'd like that very much.

She'd been so surprised at herself that she couldn't remember much else about their conversation. She'd been thinking mostly of that since, testing her new feelings over and over, as one tested a cake by sticking in a toothpick.

It was true. Sometime not so long ago, her attitude about remarrying had changed. Her heart had changed quietly and naturally, like one season melded into another, so smoothly that she'd not even noticed—until Jeremiah had brought it up.

And in a split second, standing there looking into his brown eyes, she'd realized everything had changed. She'd changed, herself.

She didn't know what to think about that.

"Everything all right?"

Susie's whisper behind her made Anna jump. The older woman stood behind her, clad in her own nightgown.

"*Ja*, Matthew's asleep." Anna stepped into the hall and pulled the door closed.

"From the look of him he'd had a busy day. That child was dirty from top to toe. I was about to make some mint tea before bed. Why don't you join me for a cup? I was hoping we could have a talk."

A talk? At this hour? Anna frowned, but she nodded. "All right."

The two women padded downstairs. The kitchen was cozy, softly lit by a gas lamp, and a faint reminder of the fried chicken they'd had for supper lingered in the air. Together the women brewed a pot of tea, and Susie placed two snickerdoodle cookies on the table with a wink.

"It's against my principles to go to bed on an empty stomach." She poured the steaming tea and settled in her chair.

Anna stirred a teaspoon of sugar into her cup, breathing in the comforting scent of mint. "What did you want to talk about, Susie? Is something bothering you?"

"Me? *Nee.* I thought maybe you'd like to talk. You've seemed…discouraged since you came home."

"I'm just tired. Mostly. It was a long day, and not as busy as I'd hoped."

"Well, you didn't have so many customers today, but it's too soon to worry about it. People will start noticing your store soon, and word gets around Hickory Springs fast. You'll have a line out the door before you know it."

Anna drew in a long breath and used it to blow on the surface of her hot tea. "Jeremiah said much the same."

"He's a *schmaert* man, Jeremiah." Susie laughed as she broke off a piece of her cookie. "Of course, I'd think anybody who agrees with me is *schmaert*." She tilted her head, studying Anna as she chewed. "A man like that would make a woman a fine husband." Susie held up one hand. "I know, you're not interested, but it's the truth, anyway."

Anna opened her mouth—then shut it. Then with no warning—and for no good reason—she burst into tears.

"Oh, my!"

Anna barely registered Susie's surprised murmur. She

covered her face with her hands, embarrassed to be acting like a silly child. Thankfully, Susie seemed to take it all in stride. The older woman scooted her chair closer and put one hand on Anna's back, rubbing in soothing circles.

"It's all right," she murmured over and over. "Everything is all right."

When Anna finally lifted her head, Susie calmly handed her a paper towel—with a few snickerdoodle crumbs stuck on it.

"Wipe your face up. There now. Feel better?" Susie asked matter-of-factly.

Anna dabbed at her eyes and nose. "A little."

"I'm going to ask you a question—and you answer me honestly, mind. Are all these waterworks because maybe—just maybe—you've realized you're not as set against marrying again as you used to be?"

Anna nodded miserably.

Susie gave a satisfied nod. "That's what I thought. Now, you drink your tea and listen to me, Anna. I've lost a husband, too, so you can believe what I'm telling you. There's nothing wrong—not one single thing—with you wanting to marry again. It's perfectly natural, and you mustn't feel guilty about it."

Guilt. Was that really what she was feeling? Anna wasn't sure. "But, you've never—" Anna thought better of finishing that sentence, but Susie, as usual, knew exactly what she meant.

"I haven't married a second time myself. That's what you're thinking." Suddenly Susie seemed very interested in brushing crumbs off the table. "You're right, of course. I haven't. Marriage teaches a woman many things. One is that it's better to have no *mann* at all than to be married to the wrong one."

Anna studied her friend with concern. She'd always assumed that Susie's marriage had been as happy as her own, and she'd certainly never heard otherwise. But this was the second time Susie had said something that made her wonder.

"That's true," Anna said slowly. "And I think that's one reason this has me feeling so unsettled. Back when Henry and I started talking about getting married, I never worried for a moment. I knew I loved him, and it all seemed so simple. But now—"

"Now you know what marriage is really like," Susie said. "The good parts of it and the hard parts, too. And of course, you've Matthew to think about, as well. It's natural you'd consider everything more carefully."

"*Ja*, that's so." It helped that Susie understood so well. "Mamm said as much, too. I can't be selfish and just choose someone who's kind to me or who I like the look of. I have to think of Matthew's future."

"Is that what she said?" Susie lifted her teacup to her lips and studied Anna over its rim. "So, is there someone? Someone who's kind, that you like the looks of?"

Jeremiah's face flashed into Anna's mind, and she was thankful that the room was dim so that Susie wouldn't see her blush. "Nobody who'd be the right choice for me."

Susie made an exasperated noise. "What makes you so sure he isn't? Oh, we both know who you're talking about, so let's stop beating about the bush. Why not Jeremiah? He's single and a very nice man."

"He is, but he's also bound and determined to farm, and you know how I feel about that."

"That does pose a problem. Unless," Susie went on hopefully, "Jeremiah doesn't end up being a farmer after all. He said himself that he wanted to try it out first before he made a commitment. Could be he'll be ready to consider some other job once his rental time is up."

"I don't know. He really seems to love farming, and that's not the life I want for Matthew. Not," she went on quickly, "that Jeremiah's made any offers. I really don't think Mamm has anything to worry about. Jeremiah's never said anything that made me think he's interested in me that way."

Susie had just taken a mouthful of her tea, and at Anna's words, she spluttered and coughed for a full minute.

"He's not said anything," she croaked out finally. "That's what you're going by? I guess he goes around building shelves and counters for all the widows in town, then? *Nee*." Susie silenced Anna's protest with a wave of her hand. "We'll not argue about it. Would you like to know if he has any interest in you? I could find out."

No doubt Susie could. She'd not gotten her reputation as a matchmaker for nothing. For years people had noticed that any time Susie Raber took a single young woman under her wing, that *maidel* was getting married before the year was out.

For a second—only for a second—Anna was tempted. But then she shook her head. "There's no point."

"Nee." Susie sipped the last of her tea thoughtfully. "Maybe not. On the other hand, you never can tell. Well, I suppose we'll just wait and see. Gott has a way of working these things out in His own good time—and He often likes to surprise us when He does."

"That's true enough." Anna picked up their empty tea-cups and started toward the sink. "But whatever Gott's got in mind for my future, He can bring about just fine without any help from you, Susie Raber. I hope you'll remember that."

She spoke politely, but firmly—and she hoped Susie knew she meant what she said.

But the only answer she got was a chuckle.

The following morning, as Jeremiah walked in from the field to get more nails from the box in the barn, a third buggy pulled up into the parking area around the Farmhouse Pantry. The trio of buggies shared the space with two Englischers' cars.

He smiled. Folks had been coming and going ever since she'd opened the doors at seven. Anna might not have had a good first day, but she was sure making up for lost time. Her customers must be keeping her busy because he'd not seen her since she'd waved at him on her way into the store.

She'd been alone this morning, and she'd worn a green dress that just matched the corn sprigs sprouting in his garden. She'd looked so fresh and pretty that he'd stumbled to a stop—and forgotten to keep walking until she'd vanished into the building.

Probably a good thing that she hadn't poked her head outside today. He'd never have gotten any work done.

As it was, he'd fought the urge to walk over and see if there was any little job she needed help with. He'd had to keep reminding himself to keep his mind—and his eyes—on his own work. That Anna Speicher had a future picked out for herself and her son that didn't include a fellow like Jeremiah Weaver.

Now that Anna had guessed about his problem with reading, she knew his limits. He didn't want her to think that he didn't recognize them himself.

Still.

He hesitated, one hand on the barn door. With so many customers—many of them carrying out bags and boxes of store goods—her shelves might be getting a little bare. She'd taken him up on the offer to store some of her extra supplies in the cellar of the house, but she could hardly run over and get anything she might need, not with a constant stream of people in and out.

He could go see. Just ask if she needed him to cart over anything while he happened to be up at the house. That would be a *freindlich* thing to do.

He glanced down at his clothes. He was dressed for fieldwork, in a stained blue shirt and a pair of pants with the knees wearing out. His clothes were streaked with dirt and sweat. He didn't much like doing laundry, so he generally waited until the weekend to do what he could with his clothing. By then, his work outfits could nearly stand up by themselves, they were so crusty.

He lifted his chin. What difference did it make? He wasn't making a social visit, nor going to church. He was offering to do a job, plain and simple. He'd loaded plenty of things into stores before, and he'd never worried what he looked like. There was no reason to start now.

No reason at all.

He walked up to the little building, standing well aside as an Englisch woman walked out with a bag full of Anna's items. She smiled at him.

"I just love your wife's store," she said cheerfully. "I'm going to tell all my friends."

She's not my wife.

He started to say that, but the woman was already nearly to her car, so he only nodded. "*Denki.* That's nice of you. Tell them they're all welcome here."

He walked into the store to find Anna's *mamm*, Mary Glick, standing just inside. She looked at him, her eyebrows raised almost to the edge of her *kapp*.

She'd overheard. He opened his mouth, but he couldn't think of any way to explain why he'd let the Englisch woman assume he and Anna were married. He cast a desperate look toward the counter, but Anna was waiting on a customer and not paying them any mind.

"Hello, Mary," he managed finally.

"Jeremiah." She eyed his dirty clothes. "You've been working hard."

"*Ja*, it's been a busy day—and not only for me. I came to ask Anna if she needed anything hauled up out of the cellar. She's had so many customers today, I figured her shelves might be getting bare."

They were, too. He saw lots of gaps where before cans and jars had been crammed together.

Mary's eyes narrowed. "Nice of you to take such an interest. *Ja*, her business has really picked up. Of course, not such a surprise considering that when I drove over to Owl Hollow this morning on an errand, nearly all the stores had flyers in their windows advertising the Farmhouse Pantry."

Jeremiah had been scanning the shelves, making mental notes of what Anna might need him to bring up from the cellar. He froze, keeping his eyes fixed on a display of spices in big jars.

"Well, that's *gut*, ain't so?" he murmured. "Whatever brings in the customers."

Before Mary could answer, Anna finished totaling up her sale. She waved at them as her customer bustled away, smiling.

"Hello, Jeremiah!" She cast a glance around at her remaining customers—who were all busily browsing the picked-over shelves—then came around the counter and headed in their direction.

"Taking a break from the vegetables?" She smiled at

him. She smelled like laundry soap and lemon today, and she looked so happy that he couldn't help but smile back.

He didn't realize until the silence had stretched out a second too long that she'd asked him a question.

"A break. *Ja.* Well, sort of."

"He's come up to see if you need any help," her mother said dryly.

"Help? With what?"

He nodded toward the shelves. "I figured your stock might need replacing. I could bring some things up from the cellar for you, if you want."

The delight in Anna's face was worth a hundred side-eyes from Mary Glick. "That would be wonderful! I've already run out of a few things. I need more of the bulk gelatin, and more wheat berries. And I think I've another box of the dehydrated blueberries down there—those have been real popular, too. And—"

"That's too much for any man to remember," Mary interrupted impatiently. "Make a list so he doesn't forget things and have to make an extra trip."

A list? Jeremiah's eyes connected with Anna's, and he tensed.

Anna started to speak, but before she could, Mary went on. "I'll go down in the cellar with him and read it off while he gathers everything up. That'll be the quickest way, and we shouldn't keep Jeremiah from his work any longer than we have to."

"Mamm, I don't know—" Anna said helplessly.

"It's all right," Jeremiah said, resigning himself to the worst. "Write out the list."

Anna threw him a worried look, but she went to the counter and scribbled some words on a piece of paper. She handed it to her mother, who scanned it, frowning.

"Miss?" An Englisch lady called from the corner of the room. "Can you tell me the difference between the hard white wheat berries and the red ones?"

"Yes, of course," Anna said. "Mamm—"

"We'll be back in a few minutes," her mother said shortly. "Come along, Jeremiah." She bustled out the door and led the way across the yard.

Jeremiah followed, feeling uneasy. When they reached the outside cellar door, he stopped and cleared his throat. "You don't have to go all the way down into the cellar, Mary. Read everything off to me once, and I'm sure I can gather the items without any trouble. I had to remember a lot of things on my delivery route, and I generally didn't make mistakes."

"Didn't you?" Mary conveyed a world of doubt with those two words. "*Nee*, I told my *dochder* I'd help you, and I will. Some folks—" her voice took a pointed tone "—believe in keeping their word. Besides, I want to talk to you."

"Oh?" Although he didn't much like the sound of that, he wasn't about to argue with Mary Glick. Resigned, he opened the outside cellar doors, exposing the old stone steps. "I'll go down first and light a lamp," he told her. "It's pretty dim down there."

"Don't worry about me. I'm sure-footed as a goat." Sure enough, she followed right behind him, waiting as he struck a match and lit the kerosene lamp kept there. The light glowed warm and bright in the cool darkness, flickering over the neat piles of Anna's supplies. The cellar smelled of earth and apples, not an unpleasant combination.

He'd thought maybe Mary would jump right into whatever she wanted to say, but instead she started reading the list, waiting between items as Jeremiah piled the things up in the center of the floor. It went quick. He'd paid attention to where he'd stowed everything, and he'd spent some time puzzling out the labels, so he'd know what was what when Anna ran short of something.

After he'd retrieved a big tub of steel-cut oats, Mary folded the list. "That's the last of it, but before we go back up I want to ask you something."

Jeremiah braced himself. Here it came. "What's that?"

"Are you really interested in this farm? Or is it my Anna you're interested in?"

"Vass?" The one word was all he could get out.

She made an impatient noise. "Don't act so *ferhoodled*. It's a fair question. Most men in this county are getting out of farming. Nowadays, with so many Englischers wanting to come by and stare at us, there's better money to be made in other ways. But you seem set on it, and now you've talked Anna into renting it instead of selling it, and then into setting up her own shop right here alongside you. And today you come along, taking time away from your own work to cart things up from the cellar for her. That doesn't sound like a wise way for a fellow to run a farm, but it might be a mighty clever way for him to win over a woman."

"That's not—I'd no idea of any such thing," Jeremiah protested clumsily.

Mary didn't look convinced, but what could he say? *I can barely read, and your daughter knows it. She's not likely to look twice at me, so it doesn't matter that I can't seem to stop looking at her.* Saying that was unlikely to make this situation any better.

"No idea?" Mary made a scoffing noise. "I'm not sure you're being truthful. Anna's a nice-looking, hardworking girl. She's a good mother, and a faithful member of the church, and she knows how to manage a house. She'd make any man a fine *fraw*."

"I don't doubt that." Talking with Mary was like one of

those Englisch highways with lots of lanes and cars switching back and forth. He'd been on one once, a long time ago, and it had made his head spin just like it was spinning now.

Mary studied him. "You know, I've heard how you treated that Esh girl over in Owl Hollow. What I haven't heard is anything about you asking for forgiveness for all the heartache and trouble you caused."

Jeremiah lifted an eyebrow. Plenty of people had dropped hints about this topic with him, especially right after it had happened, but nobody had ever been as bold as Mary. Still, maybe it was better this way—to put it all out on the table, plain instead of dealing with gossip and whispers.

"I asked for forgiveness," he told her shortly. "And I got it."

That was true. Samuel Esh had forgiven him, as best he could. Since he'd believed that Jeremiah had been the one behind the breakup, it was natural for a *daed* to struggle with forgiving such a thing. And no doubt the loss of the money laid out for the wedding and the loss of Jeremiah as a farmhand had hit hard, too.

Jeremiah didn't hold that against Samuel. He knew how hard forgiving could be.

"Well, I'm glad to hear that."

"If that's all, we'd better get these things up to Anna."

"In a minute. There's something else I'd like to know." The older woman paused a second, not taking her eyes off his face. "Can you read or not?"

"Mary?" A woman's voice floated down the cellar stairs. "Are you down there?"

Susie Raber. Jeremiah wasn't a hugging sort of man, but if Susie had been nearby, he might have made an exception. He'd never felt so relieved to be rescued from a conversation in his life.

"*Ja*, I'm helping Jeremiah," Mary called up.

Jeremiah kept his expression blank, but he thought *helping* might not be the best word.

"I've brought Matthew along," Susie called back. "And I need to get to the bakery. Anna said you were going to keep him for the rest of the workday?"

"That's right. I'll be up in a minute." Mary scooped up several of the lighter bags. "I'll carry these over to the store." As she straightened, she sent Jeremiah a thoughtful look. "You haven't answered my question."

"I can read." Honesty compelled him to add, "I'm not so *gut* at it, maybe. But I get by."

"Fair enough." Mary considered him for a minute, then sighed. "You look like you've been kicked by a mule. I hope you'll forgive me. I didn't mean to be unkind, but everybody in town is talking—about Anna having her store out here and you working the farm. Since Anna's renting a room from Susie Raber, well." Mary shrugged. "It's natural for people to suspect a match is brewing. It's plain Susie thinks well of you, but then again, Anna's not her daughter. So, I decided I'd better ask my questions, right up front."

Jeremiah nodded curtly. "Best that way. Say what you mean, so there's no confusion. Now I'll return the favor. I rented this place because I wanted to farm. Maybe there's not much money in that, but I don't need much, and I like the work. Anna's using that building for her store because it's convenient. The property still belongs to her, and the store's no bother to me. Susie has nothing to do with it, whatever folks may be thinking."

"Mary?" A thread of impatience was in Susie's voice now. "Are you coming?"

"All right, Susie! I thank you for your honesty, Jeremiah." Mary looked at him thoughtfully. "And for helping my Anna. Just so you know, I'd be happy to see her married again. Whether she knows it or not, she needs a husband, and Matthew needs a *daed*. I just pray she chooses a fellow who's able to take *gut* care of her and make her happy. My *dochder* has had more than her share of sorrow already." And with that, the older woman climbed up the stairs and vanished into the sunlight.

Jeremiah leaned over and began stacking items for easier carrying, his mind reeling. Mary Glick was a plainspoken woman for sure. He'd never had such a conversation in his life.

"Need any help?"

He glanced up to see Susie peering down at him. Without waiting for his answer, she came down the steps.

"*Denki*, if you've time for it. It'll make for fewer trips." Carefully he sorted a few lighter items to one side for Susie to take charge of.

"I'm walking back anyhow. It's no trouble to carry a little something as I go. Anyhow, it's the least I can do. I'm sorry I stole your helper."

"I'm not." The honest words popped out before he could stop them. Horrified, he froze and looked at Susie.

She chuckled. "Mary can be a little blunt sometimes, especially when she's got her feathers ruffled. What was she on about today?"

"Nothing important."

"Was she worrying you might be chasing after Anna?" When he stiffened guiltily, Susie laughed again. "Don't look so surprised. I've known Mary for years, and I know how she thinks."

"Well, she's got nothing to worry about, and I told her so."

"Did you?" Susie's voice lilted innocently on the question as she stacked the three boxes of spices he'd set aside for her. "Because it looks to me like she's not the only one wondering if this little arrangement of yours might lead to a match."

"Ja," he admitted uncomfortably. "Mary said there were folks in town saying that—especially with you being in the middle of it."

"I wasn't talking about that. Folks in town say all sorts of things, and I'm just an innocent bystander. So far, anyway. *Nee*, I was talking about Anna herself."

The wooden crate Jeremiah had just picked up hit the cellar floor with a thundering crash.

Susie chuckled again. "Well. That got your attention."

"I don't—Anna hasn't—*vass*?" Jeremiah floundered. "You can't mean that."

"Oh, I think it's early days. But I wouldn't be surprised if she wasn't starting to think about you that way, wonder a little bit. And why not? You're not married, and neither is she anymore. It's natural enough that you two should size each other up. Can you tell me you've never thought of it? You've not wondered even once if Anna Speicher might be the woman Gott's set aside for you?"

Jeremiah's head was spinning, but he had enough sense not to answer that question. "We'd best get these things over to the store. You said you needed to get to the bakery, and I've my own work to see to."

"In a minute." Susie put her hands on her hips and cocked her head to one side. "I'm making you uncomfortable. I know these things aren't usually talked about, and you've already had to deal with Mary, so my heart goes out to you. But I'd like to say my piece, too. I'll admit, I dabble in some matchmaking. Call it a little hobby—or a bad habit. I can't stand to see folks lonely when they don't have to be. And whether Anna realizes it or not, she's lonesome. Unless I miss my guess, you are, too. So? Do you like Anna or don't you?"

"I like her fine. But—"

"Then would you like me to nudge things along a little? I can't promise anything, mind you. We'll have our work cut out for us, especially with you being a farmer. Anna likes you, too, but the idea of getting married again is a new one for her, and she's made it plain she wants to be done with farm life, and with this farm in particular."

"That seems to settle it, then." Jeremiah was careful to keep his tone bland.

"Maybe. But maybe not." Susie's eyes twinkled mischievously. "In my experience funny things happen when you start telling the good Lord what you won't do. I think He likes surprising us—and teaching us Who's really in charge of things. So? Do you want my help or not?"

At least he knew the answer to that question. "*Nee.* Thank you, but I don't." He wouldn't have Anna—or any other woman—nudged in his direction, not by Susie or anybody else. The last thing he needed was a repeat of what had happened with Barbara.

Susie looked disappointed, but she nodded. "Well, that's that, I suppose. Now, I guess I'd better get going. It's nearly time for our lunch rush at the bakery."

Susie carried the boxes up the steps. She paused at the top and looked down at him. "It's your decision, of course, Jeremiah. But would you at least think about what I've said?"

"Ja." The one word was all he could manage, but it was true enough. He'd think about what she'd said.

Anna likes you, too.

In fact, he doubted he'd be able to think about anything else.

Chapter Ten

The following Tuesday, Anna was scribbling furiously on a pad, totting up a purchase while Matthew fidgeted behind the counter, impatient for his lunchtime.

The Englisch customer kept stacking items on the counter. "I'm so glad I found this place!" she exclaimed happily.

Anna laughed. "I am, too." Business had picked up beautifully over the past week. She'd been kept so busy this morning that she'd barely had time to think.

"It's a hidden gem for sure. I'd never have known about it except for the flyers I saw."

"At Smucker's Bakery? Or Yoder's Dinner Bell?"

"No, I saw the one over in Owl Hollow at Chadwick's Nursery." The woman handed over the payment with a smile.

"Owl Hollow?" That was strange. "I didn't put any flyers there." She should have, though. Chadwick's Nursery was a popular spot.

"Well, somebody did."

"Yes," another woman chimed in. "I saw one in Owl Hollow, too. At the Corner Café."

"And there was one at the hardware store and another one at that cute little cake shop," a third woman said. "They were everywhere. That's why I decided to come check the place out."

"Well, I'm happy you found me," Anna said. "And I hope you'll come back."

"Don't you worry," the first woman assured her. "This is going to be one of my regular stops."

After the women made their purchases and left, the store was empty for the first time since Anna had opened. She took a breath.

"Lunch?" asked Matthew hopefully. Susie had dropped him off earlier when she'd had to go in for her shift at the bakery. Mamm and Elizabeth were helping a neighbor today and hadn't been available to babysit.

"*Ja*, I think so." Anna hurried outside and flipped the sign over to "Closed for Lunch." Then she considered her options.

She and Matthew could certainly eat inside the store. But customers often drove up in spite of the sign, and she ended up waiting on them. And Matthew needed her attention, too.

He'd only been at the store for an hour or so, but he'd already grown bored. He'd not fussed, but instead had sat obediently at the little table she'd pulled just behind the counter and scribbled listlessly with crayons on some paper she'd given him. He'd asked to play outside, but she'd not felt comfortable allowing that, not with so many cars pulling in and out of the yard.

"We'll have a picnic," she decided. She picked up the cooler containing their lunches and led the way outside.

She paused at her buggy long enough to retrieve the old blanket she kept in the box buckled to the back. Then she led the way to a nice, shady spot under an oak not too far from the store. She spread the blanket and settled Matthew with his sandwich and some chunks of watermelon.

"*Vo is* big man?" Matthew asked around a mouthful of bread and ham.

"I don't know where he is right now. And you should call him by his name," she reminded her son. "Jeremiah."

"Jer-miah," her son repeated obediently.

Anna was privately wondering where Jeremiah was herself. She scanned the fields but saw no sign of him. She hadn't seen him all day. Chock was grazing in the pasture beside her mare, Bessie, so he hadn't left the farm.

Wherever he was, no doubt he was working. He never seemed to stop. Whenever she caught a glimpse of him through the store windows, he would be moving from one task to another. He never seemed to be in any particular hurry, but there was no doubt he got things done.

The big produce garden looked good, best she could tell from here. Second summer crops were unpredictable. There were more insects this time of year, and the weather sometimes heated up too fast for the plants to do well, and of course, keeping everything watered was a challenge. And she'd only had a family-sized plot to manage, not one so big as that one.

But Jeremiah's garden was greening up nicely, and the seedlings seemed to be coming along well. She just hoped he was being careful, not tiring himself out too much. It was early days—the garden would need even more work as time went by.

"There! There the big man!" Matthew pointed with one sticky finger. Anna turned her head, and her heart lifted.

Sure enough, Jeremiah was walking up from the bottom field. He was carrying a hoe and a handsaw, and Sunny the dog trotted at his heels, her ears and tail at happy angles. She wasn't the only happy one—Matthew stood up and waved for all he was worth, bouncing with excitement.

The movement must have caught Jeremiah's eye because

he smiled and waved back. "Hello!" he called. "Taking a lunch break?"

"We are. And we've extra, if you'd like some!" Anna called back.

Jeremiah didn't answer until he'd closed most of the gap between them. He scanned their little setup, his smile warming when Matthew ran over to give Sunny a hug.

"You've got yourself set up nice. It's a *gut* spot for a picnic."

"Then why don't you join us?" she asked. "We've got plenty, as you can see for yourself." She gestured at the extra sandwich and the plastic container still half-full of watermelon.

"I wouldn't want to pester," he said uncomfortably.

"Don't be silly. I'm glad for the company." And she was, she realized. In fact, she felt almost ridiculously glad to see him. "Have a seat."

Jeremiah cast a worried look toward the road. Where they were sitting, they were shielded from the view of most passersby. It was one reason she'd picked this spot, so she wouldn't be easily spotted by customers.

"I suppose it's all right," he said cautiously. "*Denki.* Let me get some water for Sunny, and I'll be back."

"I go, too!" Matthew announced—but he cast a hopeful look toward Anna as he spoke. He'd lately taken to telling her what he was going to do rather than asking for permission. It wasn't something she wanted to encourage but, of course, it was all part of growing up.

"May I go?" she reminded him quietly.

"May go? With big—Jer-miah?" The child corrected himself quickly.

"It's okay by me." Jeremiah glanced down at the boy with a smile that twisted Anna's heart into a painful knot.

"All right," she managed. "But mind you don't get your-self wet." She watched them go, the man so tall that he had to stoop a little to tousle her son's hair, his hand nearly as big as the child's head. Even though Matthew was a good size for his age, he looked impossibly tiny next to Jeremiah.

Tiny and very safe.

It wasn't easy being a single parent, even with a com-munity of loving adults around you, ready to step in when you needed an extra pair of hands. It was still her respon-sibility to take care of Matthew. After losing Henry so un-expectedly, keeping Matthew safe was something Anna had to work hard not to worry too much about. Especially now that they were spending so much time on the farm.

Except when Matthew was with Jeremiah. It was partly because of his size, she supposed. Jeremiah looked so big and strong, and he clearly had a soft spot for Matthew. But whatever the reason, when she saw her tiny son walking beside Jeremiah, a load lifted off her heart.

"Mamm! I helped!" Matthew raced back across the yard, obviously excited.

"He helped fill Sunny's bowl." Jeremiah nodded over his shoulder where the little dog was lapping up water, her tail wagging. "But I kept a watch so he didn't get very wet."

There were some damp spatters darkening Matthew's pants, but not too many. "It looks like you both did a *gut* job. Now have a seat and eat some lunch."

Jeremiah chose a spot where he could lean against the trunk, stretching his long legs off to the side, out of the way. He accepted the food she offered with thanks and bowed his head for a silent prayer before digging in.

He had nice hair, Jeremiah did, Anna thought idly. Thick

and dark with a little bit of a wave to it when it was damp—like it was now. He must have tried to clean himself up a little at the pump.

She wouldn't call him handsome, exactly. His nose was a little crooked, as if maybe it had been broken sometime, and there were sun-squint lines around his eyes, and his jaw was very square.

Jeremiah looked like the sort of man a person could trust, the type who would tackle the hard parts of life without having to be asked or prodded. And as near as she could tell, that was exactly the kind of fellow he was.

He glanced up as he took his first bite of the sandwich and caught her looking. She flushed and quickly shifted her gaze to Sunny. She shouldn't stare at the poor man while he was trying to eat his lunch.

The dog had rejoined them and sat politely at the edge of the blanket, obviously hoping that a scrap of sandwich would come her way. Matthew sat between the dog and Jeremiah, one hand on Jeremiah's knee, the other stroking the dog's head as he chattered softly to her. Occasionally, the dog gave the child a maternal lick on the cheek.

There was something about it—seeing the three of them sitting there so relaxed and at ease together, that made a lump form in Anna's throat.

"You might have to get a dog," Jeremiah said—in Englisch so the child wouldn't understand. Since he wasn't school age yet, Matthew still spoke only Deutsch.

Anna blinked and managed a smile. "Susie might have something to say about that. For now maybe we'd better just share yours."

"Sunny doesn't seem to mind," Jeremiah said.

Just then, Matthew leaned forward to hug the patient dog, for all the world as if he'd understood what they'd been talking about. Jeremiah chuckled and glanced at Anna, and their eyes met—and held.

An ordinary moment in the middle of a busy summer day. They weren't talking about anything in particular, and there was nothing special going on.

Or there hadn't been—until now.

As Jeremiah looked into her eyes, his jaw frozen in mid-chew as if he couldn't move, a little flutter started in the pit of Anna's stomach. The rest of the world melted away as she focused on the feeling. She hadn't felt that special flutter in a very long time, but she recognized it all the same.

She'd felt much the same way when Henry had first caught her eye across the table at a singing. She'd felt like he was asking her something, but without saying a word.

She felt the same way now. But surely... Jeremiah couldn't be...

"Anna." Jeremiah's voice sounded strange.

"Ja?"

"I think—" He swallowed. "You've got a customer driving up."

"Oh!"

And just like that, the everyday world came rushing back in. The sound of a buggy pulling into the drive, the smell of watermelon—and slightly damp dog. The soft weave of the blanket she'd unconsciously wadded up in her fingers.

She looked over her shoulder to see Trudy Schwartz waving from her buggy. Oh, dear. Even from this distance she could see how the other woman's eyes lingered on Jeremiah.

"Looks like I do." Anna rose hastily to her feet, dusting breadcrumbs off her apron. "I guess that means it's time to go to work! Matthew, come along. We need to get back to the store."

"I help big—Jer-miah," Matthew suggested, his blue

eyes hopeful. "May I," the little boy corrected quickly. "May I, Mamm?"

Before Anna could answer, another buggy pulled in, followed by a blue car driven by an elderly Englisch woman.

"Looks like you're going to be busy, and I don't have much to do this afternoon." Jeremiah hadn't budged from his spot, half the sandwich seemingly forgotten in one hand. "Nothing the boy can't tag along with, anyhow. He can keep the *hund* entertained."

"Anna?" Trudy had started across the yard. In another minute, she'd be over here, no doubt flirting for all she was worth.

Suddenly Anna didn't like that idea at all.

"All right," she agreed recklessly. "If you're sure you don't mind. Keep an eye on him, please. If he gets in the way, just bring him back to the store." She started across the yard to intercept Trudy. "And *denki*!" she called back over her shoulder.

As Anna approached, Trudy halted. Her face was a picture of disappointment—mixed with a touch of envy. But when Anna reached her, she smiled.

"Well!" she said as they walked toward the store where the other customers were waiting. "You and Jeremiah sure looked nice and cozy. If I didn't know better, I'd think there was something sparking between you two."

"Don't be silly," Anna said breezily. "We were just grabbing a quick lunch. Come on inside, Trudy. I have more of those dried dates you wanted."

"Do you?" Trudy asked absently. She glanced over her shoulder and sighed sadly. "So that's all it was? Just a quick lunch? I'm not so sure I believe that."

Anna managed a laugh, but she didn't answer. Because all of a sudden, she wasn't so sure she believed that, either.

* * *

"They growing!" Matthew chattered happily in Deutsch, pointing to the bean sprouts that were flourishing in the garden. "There! And there! Look, Big Jer-miah!"

"I see!" Jeremiah grinned at his new nickname. It didn't bother him. Being taller than most fellows never had. But he imagined Anna might have something to say when she heard it.

He glanced over toward the store building for the dozenth time that afternoon. Although the wind was blowing in the opposite direction—and it was too far anyway—he almost thought he caught a whiff of laundry soap and vanilla.

His grin broadened, and his insides started churning, all warm and soft—like a batch of fudge bubbling on a cookstove. Ever since that unexpected picnic, his stomach had been doing some funny things—and he couldn't seem to keep his mind where it ought to be.

"Big Jer-miah! Look!" Matthew was jumping up and down with excitement. He'd discovered a tiny bloom on one of the biggest bean plants. "Flower!"

"*Ja*, that's *gut*. It means we'll have beans before too long."

"*Gut!*" Matthew put his hands on his hips, threw back his shoulders and barked a triumphant laugh at the blue sky. "Ha! Beans!" he shouted.

Jeremiah laughed along with him. He understood exactly how the little boy felt. He doubted the child really loved vegetables that much. This was the happy triumph of the farmer, the joy of seeing the plants under his care growing well and doing what they were supposed to do.

He felt that way, too. Every morning he gave thanks to Gott for the opportunity to live and work here.

Matthew's energy got the better of him. He ran down the

path between the bean rows, laughing and jumping into the air about every third step, his blond hair gleaming bright in the hot midday sun.

Jeremiah didn't blame him. If he wasn't a grown man, he might have done the same thing.

He didn't know if he could be successful as a farmer. Not yet. But he did know beyond the shadow of a doubt that this was what he wanted—with all of his heart. So much that it nearly brought him to his knees to think of it.

He wanted this. This, right here. This land, this life.

This family.

Jeremiah halted halfway down the row, his hoe forgotten in his hand. He tested the thought, his pulse pounding, as he watched Matthew pick up a stick at the edge of the field and start poking in the dirt with it. Sunny barked at him, keeping a cautious distance, her tail wagging.

Ja, Jeremiah realized. It was true.

He didn't just want the Speicher farm anymore. He wanted the Speichers. He wanted Anna and Matthew for his own, too.

With all his heart. So much it nearly brought him to his knees to think of it.

He resumed walking slowly, scratching at the few weeds between the plants as he went, turning this over in his mind.

He'd admired Anna all along. Thought she was real pretty. On the outside, of course, but anybody with a working pair of eyes could see that. But it turned out, she was pretty on the inside, too. Sweet and full of spunk and so *schmaert*. A loving *mamm*. And he'd thought Matthew was a fine little boy, too. Cute and healthy and bright.

Of course, he hadn't ever expected a woman like Anna would admire him back. And maybe deep down in the cellar of his heart, he'd been a little regretful over that. But only a little. He'd learned long ago not to butt his head against the gates Gott set up. Besides, he was reaching far enough past his comfort zone, just trying for the farm.

But this, now...

This was a different feeling altogether, different even from how he'd felt about Barbara. This wasn't so much a hope or a dream as a desperate, fierce longing—the way a man longed for water after a long, hot and dusty day.

Nee, it was more than that. It was the way a man longed for air.

He watched Matthew playing with his stick at the edge of the field, and he recalled the conversations he'd had with Mary Glick and Susie in the farmhouse cellar.

He'd thought about what they'd said, sure, especially that part about Anna liking him. But liking wasn't the same as loving. Women often played guessing games when it came to folks pairing up, and they weren't always right. Any future with Anna in it, he'd decided, was too much for a man like him to hope for.

But today, when they'd been sitting together under that old tree, there'd been a minute where he'd wondered— where it had seemed like Anna really was looking at him different. Like maybe this wasn't too much for him to hope for, after all.

Too much to hope for or not, he was hoping now—and hoping hard.

The question was—what was he going to do about it? How—

A scream interrupted Jeremiah's thoughts, jarring him so much that his hoe slipped and sliced off a bean plant, right at ground level.

He whipped around, shading his eyes against the sun. Matthew was hopping up and down and screaming—not with joy now, but in fear and pain. Sunny was jumping and yelping, too. Whatever was hurting Matthew was hurting the dog as well, but she wouldn't leave his side.

Jeremiah took off at a run, closing the gap between himself and the boy as fast as he could. "Matthew! Run here! Run to me!"

Matthew paid no attention. The child was too upset to obey, and now that Jeremiah was closer, he could see why.

Bees. Some type of bees. The boy was slapping at the air and shrieking as a line of angry insects boiled up from a hole in the ground beside him—around the stick Matthew had innocently stuck into their nest.

Yellow jackets, must be. By the time Jeremiah realized that, he'd made it to the child. He threw down the hoe and snatched Matthew up. He cradled the struggling boy in his arms, hunching his body around him as he ran back across the field. Sharp, hot stings burned on his back and neck. Yellow jackets weren't forgiving creatures, and when they were provoked, they gave chase.

Matthew's shrieking didn't slow down, and neither did Jeremiah. He stayed at a full run until he reached Chock's water trough, freshly filled that morning. He dropped the child in with a splash and began stripping off the boy's clothes.

He was still getting stung himself, and he slapped furiously at the flying pests, crushing them before they could find Matthew. The boy's screams died down to snuffling sobs as Jeremiah checked him over, murmuring as calmly as he could.

"It's all right. I know it hurts. We'll fix it. Where did they get you?" Two stings. No, three. That was all he could find, but they were swelling up, making big and angry red welts.

Jeremiah's pounding heart slowed. Not so bad. Only three.

He felt another burning sting on his neck. He picked up a handy bucket, dipped it in the trough and poured it over his head.

"Vass is letz?" He heard Anna's desperate cry and looked over to see her running in his direction. "What's happened?"

"He's all right! He got stung."

Anna reached the trough and pulled her son up, checking him over with frantic hands. "Are you all right, Matthew? Where does it hurt you?"

"He's got three stings that I can see." An idea occurred to him, and his heart stalled. "He's not allergic is he? To yellow jacket stings?"

Anna didn't answer. She was shaking. Her whole body trembled as she pulled her child against her, holding him tight. Three women—one Amish and two Englisch—had come out of the store and stood beside it staring at them.

"Should I call an ambulance?" one of them shouted.

"Matthew," Anna murmured over and over as her son snuffled against her.

"Anna." Jeremiah spoke sharply. He had to get her attention. "Is the boy allergic to yellow jackets?"

The sharpness worked. She blinked and shook her head. *"Nee.* Not allergic."

Jeremiah's breath rushed out. *"Ach,* that's *gut.* It's all right!" he shouted back to the woman by the store. She had a phone in her hand. "No ambulance needed!"

"All right?" Anna looked up at him, her face white and her blue eyes wide and blank with fear—and anger. "There's nothing all right here! You were supposed to be looking after him! I trusted you!"

"*Ja,* I'm sorry." Jeremiah's relief sank into guilt at the accusing look in Anna's face. "He was at the edge of the field. With a stick. I got to him as fast as I could, but—"

"Anna?" The Plain woman—Trudy, that was her name—called from up the hill. "Are you sure everything's all right?"

"Matthew's hurt, Trudy!" Anna lifted her son into her arms, water darkening her dress.

Trudy had a quick aside with the Englisch women, shooing them toward their cars, and then she started their way.

"Let me carry him," Jeremiah offered.

"*Nee.*" Anna spoke the word shortly. "I'll do it."

She turned and started up the hill, meeting her friend halfway. The two women hovered over the boy, walking up the hill, talking to each other.

Jeremiah stood dripping beside the trough, watching them walk away. He looked down at Sunny. One side of her snout was swelling, and the stings on his own body were welting up, as well. Too many of them to count. He was in for an unpleasant few days.

Not that it mattered, so long as the boy was all right.

Sunny was gazing after Anna and Matthew. Trudy was helping them into her buggy, no doubt having offered to drive them home. The dog whined pitifully, and Jeremiah gently fondled her head.

"Not your fault, Sunny. You did everything you could. It's all right."

The dog looked sadly up at him. She lay down, plopped her nose on her lopsided snout and heaved a heavy sigh as if she didn't believe him.

"*Ja.*" Jeremiah answered with a deep sigh of his own. "I know just how you feel."

Chapter Eleven

The following morning, when Anna dropped Matthew off at her sister's home for the day, she set a jar of medicated salve on the kitchen counter.

"What's that?" Elizabeth was busy washing breakfast dishes, her seven-year-old daughter, Abigail, drying them carefully.

"It's for his bee stings."

"Oh, I have plenty of salve." Elizabeth scrubbed hard at a skillet. "With so many *kinder* around, we're dealing with insect bites all the time in summer. Take that with you and keep it at the store. No doubt you'll need it again."

Anna stayed silent, but Matthew wouldn't be going back out to the farm. Not anytime soon, not if she could help it. Yesterday, hearing her child screaming from the very same field where his *daed* had died—that wasn't an experience she ever wanted to repeat.

She wasn't sure how she was going to manage, though. Elizabeth, Mamm and Susie were cheerfully trading Matthew among themselves, but there were still times when nobody was available to babysit.

And there was another problem.

As she bent to hug her son goodbye, Matthew looked up at her, his bottom lip pooched out. He didn't fuss. She'd talked to him firmly on the buggy ride over and made it clear that he wasn't to pester her any more about going to the farm. But he clearly wasn't happy.

Once the stings had stopped hurting, he'd told her the story, as best he could. It was plain that—in Matthew's mind at least—Jeremiah was a hero.

Bad bugs bite! Big Jer-miah come and grab me up! He run and run and frow me in the trough! In my clothes!

Her little boy considered that part very funny, and he always laughed out loud.

Anna didn't find it funny at all. The fact was, Matthew was still a very young child, and he'd been allowed to get far enough away from Jeremiah that he'd gotten hurt.

It wasn't Jeremiah's job to look after Matthew, of course. It was hers, so mostly this was her own fault. She never should have allowed this arrangement in the first place, and honestly, she wasn't sure why she had.

She wouldn't make the same mistake again.

When Anna walked outside, she saw a familiar Englisch car pulling up. Kayla Kennedy, one of her family's favorite drivers, hopped out of the blue convertible and waved enthusiastically.

"You're driving your own car today?" Anna called. Often Kayla drove her mother's minivan to ferry their Amish friends to various appointments.

"It's only your mama today," the twenty-six-year-old Englischer responded cheerfully. "So we don't need much room. I'm really glad I caught you, though. I wanted to ask you about something."

"What's that?" Anna tried not to sound impatient. She didn't like the idea of opening her store late, and her Plain customers tended to be early birds. Driving Matthew all the way out here had already taken a good chunk of her morning.

"You know about the tours I give during the summer, right?"

Anna nodded. "Yes, for people who want to learn about Plain life."

During the school year, Kayla taught language arts at the local middle school. A couple of years ago, she'd approached her Amish friends and asked permission to bring her students along to their farm on a field trip so they could understand their Plain neighbors better.

Everyone liked Kayla and trusted her to be respectful, so permission had been readily granted, and the tours had become a regular thing. Recently Kayla had begun offering them for adults, as well.

"Right," Kayla was saying. "So, I heard about your new store out at the farm, and I wondered if you'd be all right with me making it the final stop on my tours. A lot of the women have asked about buying items at an authentic Amish grocery." She laughed. "I don't think they realize you guys shop in a lot of the same places we do. But from what I've heard about your place, they'd love it, and they'd probably spend a good bit of money there, too. I'm up to three tours a week most weeks, so it will bring you in some business, if you're interested."

"Oh, that would be wonderful!" Anna sent a silent prayer of repentance for being impatient. Kayla was doing her a big favor.

"I know it's short notice, but I have a tour this Friday, if that will work."

"It will," Anna assured her firmly.

"Great!" Kayla flipped her wrist and checked her watch. "I'd better go knock on the door of the *dawdi haus* and let your *mamm* know I'm here."

"*Dawdi haus* and *mamm*?" Anna's mood, which hadn't

been so happy since the yellow jacket incident, had lifted. "Be careful, Kayla! You're starting to sound Plain!"

Kayla laughed as she started across the yard. "There are worse things to be."

Anna had reached her buggy when an idea occurred to her. "Kayla," she called. "How did you find out about my store? Did Mamm tell you?"

Kayla halted on the porch steps. "No, it was your friend, that big Amish guy, Jeremiah. He used to make deliveries all over Owl Hollow, so the storekeepers were happy to put up your flyers when he asked. I was showing around a tour when he was taping one up in a window. When I stopped to look, he handed me one and promised me my Englisch ladies would love your store. Let's hope he's right! See you on Friday!"

Anna climbed into her buggy, thinking hard. So, Jeremiah had been the one posting the flyers in all the Owl Hollow stores. Since he wasn't making deliveries now, he'd likely made a special trip to do it. More than that, he'd talked Kayla into bringing her tours to the store, as well.

That was a very nice thing to do. No doubt Susie and Mamm would have their own ideas about why Jeremiah had gone to such trouble.

And maybe they weren't so far off, after all. Anna's mind circled back to that moment under the oak tree, to those long seconds when she'd lost herself looking into Jeremiah's eyes—and to the unspoken question she thought she'd seen there.

She didn't know what that meant, but she wasn't so sure she could say now that he'd never shown any special interest in her. But even if she'd misread that look, the man had offered her nothing but kindness. And yesterday she'd been anything but kind in return.

Matthew getting hurt on the farm—even a little—had been her worst fear coming true. And Matthew could have been stung far worse if Jeremiah hadn't acted so fast.

She thought things over as she drove the horse down the quiet highway. By the time she reached the farm, she'd come to a decision. She owed Jeremiah an apology.

Not because she was looking for more than friendship, she assured herself. It was simply that she'd been sharp-tongued with a man who'd done his best to help her, even when it wasn't his responsibility to do so. He'd been kind to Matthew, too. Maybe he should have been watching the child more closely, but it wasn't his fault the boy got stung, and he'd done all he could.

She drove the buggy into the yard and hopped down. She planned to quickly unhitch and turn her mare into the pasture with Chock. Then she'd find Jeremiah and mend her fences with him as best she could. She did hope he wasn't working on the far part of the farm, though, because she needed to check over her stock before she opened and maybe bring a few more things up from the cellar.

She'd just reached for the harness when Jeremiah came out of the barn.

"I can do that," he offered gruffly.

Anna glanced over, poised to make the apology she'd been practicing in her mind. But at the sight of him, every word went right out of her head.

Jeremiah looked terrible. His face was swollen with half a dozen angry welts, and several more were visible on his forearms.

"Oh, no!" She left Bessie standing in harness and walked toward him, scanning the stings. So many of them. "Oh, Jeremiah. Look at you."

"*Ja*, I know." He shifted uncomfortably. "I'm something

to look at, certain sure. But it's no matter." An anxious look crossed his mottled face. "How's Matthew doing? Is he all right?"

"He's fine. He wasn't stung too much. How many times did they get you?"

"I didn't count 'em. Mostly what you can see, and a good many more on my back. I'm glad the little one's all right. I've been worried." His face had brightened. "That's a relief."

"Jeremiah." Anna stopped, struck speechless by her own selfishness. How could she not even have thought of this? Of course he'd gotten stung—and badly—racing to Matthew and getting him out of the field. And she'd not even asked him, not offered him any help. She'd only fussed at him and blamed him for letting Matthew get stung. "That's not the only relief you need. You must be so uncomfortable!"

He put a finger inside the neck of his shirt and shifted it. "I've felt better, but I'll get by. This heat's not helping, but I don't feel as rough as I did last night, so that's something, I guess. The main thing is that your boy isn't bad hurt." He walked to her horse and began the process of unbuckling the straps. "I'll see to your horse so you can get the store opened up."

She followed him. "I'm so sorry, Jeremiah."

He looked at her over his shoulder. "I'm the one who's sorry. You're right, I should've been keeping a better eye. If I'd been closer, I'd have stopped him from poking his stick in that hole, or at the least, I might could have gotten him clear before they started stinging."

"It's not your fault!" The guilt and shame she felt made her voice sharper than she meant for it to be. "I'm the one who should be asking forgiveness. You were only watching Matthew as a favor to me, and one I had no right to ask."

"You didn't ask, as I recall. I offered." He had the horse free from the buggy, and he walked her over to the pasture gate and turned her loose. "And I was glad to do it. Spending time with Matthew is no chore to me. I enjoy it."

"Do you enjoy posting flyers about my store, too? I hear you've been putting them up all over Owl Hollow, which explains why my business has been doing so much better lately."

Jeremiah rubbed the back of his neck and winced. "That was no trouble. I know a lot of the storekeepers there. Some won't put up flyers for just anybody, but if they know you, they're more willing. So, I took a few of yours and scattered 'em around. That's all."

"You also talked Kayla Kennedy into giving my store a spot on her tours."

Jeremiah shrugged—and winced again. "That was just talking. I've seen her bringing Englisch ladies around Owl Hollow. She's always looking for new places because she's got some who like to do the tours over again." He frowned. "You don't mind, do you? They spend a lot of money, those ladies, and they're real polite."

"Mind? No, I don't mind. I'm thankful, Jeremiah. And I'm sorry that I didn't take more care with my words when Matthew was stung. I shouldn't have blamed you."

"I don't know about that."

"Well, I do. Matthew's been going on and on about how Big Jer-miah saved him, and he's right. Not," she added hastily, "about the nickname. I'll speak to him about that."

"I wish you wouldn't. Being called big doesn't bother me any."

"Maybe not, but those bites must be bothering you plenty. Wait there." She ran back to her buggy to retrieve the jar of salve her sister had refused.

She offered it to him. "This will help the swelling and the itching."

He examined the jar. "*Denki.* I appreciate it."

"Consider it a peace offering. Did you really mean what you said? About Matthew not being a bother to you?"

"*Ja,* sure, I meant it. The boy can call me Big Jer-miah or whatever else he likes."

"That's not what I meant. I was asking you if you were being honest when you said you enjoyed spending time with him. Or were you just being polite?"

Jeremiah looked up. "I wasn't being polite. I wouldn't have said I liked spending time with your boy if I didn't. Why?"

"Well, on the days the tours come by, I'm going to be extra busy. Mamm or Susie may be able to keep Matthew with them, but now and again, I'll have to bring him to the store. If you're working close by, would you mind letting him hang around with you? Just while the tours are here?"

That was another decision she'd come to on the ride over, and seeing the price Jeremiah was willing to pay to protect Matthew had cemented her resolve. Matthew would be fine, she told herself. She couldn't wrap him in cotton wool forever.

Jeremiah studied her, absently turning the little jar round and round in his hands. "You trust me to watch him again?"

"I do." Mostly. She pushed her worries to the back of her mind. "I'm sure you'll take *gut* care of him."

"I will." He spoke so strongly that she didn't doubt him for a minute. "I'll keep him right by me, every minute. *Denki,* Anna."

"For the salve? You're welcome. I hope it helps. Now, I'd better get to work!"

She smiled quickly and turned away before he could tell her that he hadn't been thanking her for the salve at all.

She knew that. What she didn't know was why seeing this man's not-so-handsome face, red and swollen with stings, light up over the idea of having her two-year-old tagging along on his chores had her blinking back tears.

Susie and Mamm would probably have had their own ideas about that, too.

A few weeks later, Jeremiah stood in the farmhouse kitchen, trying his best to look trustworthy. Judging by the uncertain expression on Anna's face, he wasn't doing so *gut*. It was Wednesday, a tour bus day, and for the first time nobody else had been available to keep Matthew.

"Are you sure you don't mind looking after him this afternoon?" she asked.

"Positive." Jeremiah winked at the little boy, who was sitting at the kitchen table finishing up his lunch. "I'm looking forward to it."

Over the last couple of weeks, he and Anna had fallen into the habit of having lunch together. He'd invited her to start eating inside so that she could close up the store and not be bothered by customers. Now that people had found out about the Farmhouse Pantry, Anna hardly had a minute to spare from the time she opened until the time she closed up shop.

Shortly after she'd given him the bee sting salve—which had worked wonders—he'd walked up to the store at the end of the day to return the jar. Anna had been busy waiting on customers, but Susie Raber had drawn him aside.

"I wish," she'd said, "that you'd invite Anna to eat her lunch in your kitchen on the days she works here. Even if she locks the door during her lunchtime, people knock and pester her to open. She doesn't feel right ignoring them, especially with them peering in the windows at her. If she had someplace else to eat—"

"Of course she can come up to the house." He should have thought of that himself. "I can make myself scarce and have my lunch later."

"Oh, *nee*, that won't work at all," Susie had argued. "If she has any idea that she's inconveniencing you, she'll never agree to it. You just have your lunch at your usual time. Maybe even let her share some things with you—I'll make sure she has extra. That way she won't feel guilty about intruding."

Jeremiah had shot Susie a suspicious look. A fellow didn't have to be able to read well to be able to read between the lines here.

She'd flapped her hand and made an exasperated noise. "Oh, for pity's sake, Jeremiah. Just ask her."

So, he had. He hadn't expected Anna to agree, but to his surprise, she did, and the lunch hour had quickly become his favorite part of the day.

Before, it had only been a nuisance, and he'd put off stopping work until the gnawing in his middle got too bothersome to ignore. Now he found himself watching the sun, impatient for the moment Anna would slip out of the store and walk toward the farmhouse, swinging her lunch cooler in one hand.

"Well, if you're sure you don't mind having Matthew underfoot, it'll be a big help," she said now, rising and beginning to clear up the table. "Tour days are so busy. Not," she added with a laugh, "that I'm complaining, mind you. I'm thankful for the business." She carried their glasses over to the sink and leaned forward to peek out the window. "It looks like rain. I hope that won't stop the ladies from coming."

"It won't," he assured her. "Might even make 'em stay longer. In Owl Hollow on rainy days, they'd often end up milling around a store well past closing time."

Anna glanced back at him, her face brightening with a smile. "I hope so. The longer they browse the more they spend. But then, Matthew—"

"He'll be fine. I'll keep a close eye." The reminder of the threatening rain made him reach for the paper he'd stashed in his pocket. He glanced apprehensively in Anna's direction, but she was busy washing dishes and was paying him no attention. She hummed as she worked.

He'd offered to help, but she'd refused the offer with a cheerful smile. "I know my way around a kitchen," she'd told him. "This one in particular."

That was true, of course. Maybe he should have argued more, but he found he liked watching her work. She moved quietly and briskly around the kitchen, neatening things up, putting things away. There was no doubt that since they'd started their daily lunches together, the kitchen looked— and smelled—a lot fresher.

It was nice, that. And when he came in from the fields in the evening, dog-tired and sweaty, the clean kitchen felt like a kiss on the cheek. As if somebody cared.

He looked down at his hands, folded on the table—hands he'd spent some extra time scrubbing before coming inside. He was more convinced than ever that Susie's suggestion about these lunches had something to do with her matchmaking. She shouldn't be meddling, but the woman certain sure knew her business—at least the part about getting a fellow to care about a girl. Not that he'd needed much nudging from Susie for that.

He couldn't tell if Susie's matchmaking worked as well the other way. Sometimes he thought maybe Anna looked at him a little different these days, but other times he wasn't so sure. And he still couldn't wrap his mind around the possibility that she could ever really—

"Jeremiah?"

Anna was looking at him, amusement on her face. She must have been talking, and he'd missed it.

"Vass?"

"I said, I was about to go open the store for the afternoon. But would you like me to take a look at that paper first? The one you have hidden in your pocket?"

He froze guiltily. "It's nothing. Only the tag off a fertilizer bag I bought in town. I was just studying up, seeing about how best to put it out on my corn."

"You're having trouble reading it," she said matter-of-factly. She dried her fingers on the towel, walked over and held out her hand. "Why don't I read it to you?"

He drew the paper out of his pocket. "I can read it."

"I know." She wiggled her fingers. "But I can do it faster, and you're going to be slowed down enough this afternoon." She nodded toward Matthew, who was trying to fit half a chocolate chip cookie in his mouth. "Let me help you like you're helping me."

Jeremiah couldn't see his way clear to argue about that, so he reluctantly handed the paper over. Anna read the instructions aloud quickly.

"Do you need me to read it again?" she asked when she'd finished.

"Nee." He rarely needed things told to him twice. *"Denki.* I wasn't sure whether it was best to put it out before the rain or after. Sounds like before is best, so I'll see to that. Matthew can tag along. I'll keep him close, but I'll be careful not to let him touch the fertilizer," he added.

Anna nodded, but a worry line creased her forehead.

"All right," she said. "Well, I'd best be getting to the store. You be a good boy, Matthew, and don't give Jeremiah any trouble."

She walked halfway to the door and stopped.

"Jeremiah," she said, an odd note in her voice.

"Ja?" He braced himself. Here it came, he figured. She'd changed her mind and realized she wasn't willing to trust him with her son after all.

"I want you to know, if you ever need help—with reading papers and things like that—just tell me. It was hard for me, too, at first, after Henry died. To be honest with people about how I was really feeling and what needed doing. But if I can learn to do that, you can, too."

She left the kitchen without waiting for an answer. Jeremiah sat in the quiet room, watching Matthew finish his cookie, looking at the freshly washed glasses turned upside down in the drainer. The scent of her soap still hung in the air.

Honest. Anna thought he should be honest with her.

"Out?" Matthew had finished his cookie and was tugging on Jeremiah's sleeve. "Out now?"

Jeremiah blinked. "You're right. We have work to do." He pushed back from the table. "That rain's not going to hold off for long." And no fertilizer would get spread with him sitting in the house daydreaming about Anna.

He and Matthew worked in the fields for two hours or so, Jeremiah fertilizing the corn by hand as Matthew and Sunny tagged behind. The coming storm had made things muggy and hot and by the time they'd reached the last hills of corn, both he and the boy were sweaty.

The rain broke just as they finished, coming down in sheets. Jeremiah dropped the empty fertilizer bucket, swept Matthew up into his arms and sprinted for the barn. He ran as fast as he'd run from the yellow jackets, and Matthew shrieked just as loud—but this time, with laughter.

They were soaked when they reached the shelter of the old building, but Jeremiah had a clean towel stowed in his buggy, and he dried Matthew off while the child giggled.

Yawning, the little boy plopped down on a pile of clean straw Jeremiah had heaped against one weathered wall. Sunny shook herself, spraying water everywhere, and then she joined him, curling up with a tired sigh. By the time Jeremiah had dried himself off and draped the towel over the back of the buggy seat, both the boy and the dog were fast asleep.

Jeremiah busied himself in the barn for a few minutes, doing odds and ends. But there wasn't much that needed doing, not inside anyway, and the trouble he'd had sleeping lately was catching up with him. The rain pattered down on the tin roof of the barn in a steady, soothing rhythm, and the air had turned deliciously cool.

This heavy rain wouldn't last long. Maybe it wouldn't hurt to rest just a minute. He settled himself in the straw next to Sunny and allowed himself a luxurious stretch. He gently rested one hand on Matthew's shoulder, so that he'd know if the boy woke up.

Then he drew in a long, weary breath and closed his eyes.

Anna stood in the barn doorway, looking at the scene in front of her. Matthew and Jeremiah were sound asleep, nestled in a pile of clean straw. Sunny lay between them, her head resting on Matthew's knee. The dog cracked open one eye to look at Anna, and her tail twitched in a tiny wag.

They looked awfully comfortable. Anna glanced around the barn, cool and dim on this rainy afternoon. The tools

Henry tended to lean against the walls were now hung up on wooden pegs. Even as busy as Jeremiah had been lately, the stalls had been mucked out, and the place smelled more of sunbaked straw than manure.

As much as she'd loved Henry—and she had—he'd never kept the barn so clean. There was just never enough time in the day for all the chores that needed doing.

No wonder Jeremiah was tired.

Anna studied his face, relaxed in sleep. Straw chaff littered his dark hair, and he was snoring softly. He looked worn out. In spite of the steady stream of treats Susie had been sending, his cheeks were leaner and tanned from working in the summer sun.

One muscled arm was draped over Matthew's shoulders so protectively that a lump formed in Anna's throat. The sight gave her the funniest feeling—as if she wanted to smile and cry at the same time.

Suddenly Jeremiah opened his eyes and blinked. He turned his head to check on Matthew, then moved his arm, gently, so as not to wake the boy up. Matthew sighed, snuggled a little deeper into the straw and kept sleeping.

Jeremiah rose to his feet, brushing straw off his clothing. He offered Anna a sheepish grin, but his eyes were worried as he walked closer.

"I'm sorry," he said softly. "I really was keeping an eye on him, although I'm sure it doesn't much look like it. I'd have felt it if he stirred."

"*Nee*, that's all right," she assured him quickly. "You were both so tired. It's no wonder you fell asleep." They looked at the straw pile where Matthew still slept, Sunny curled protectively next to him. "He looks so comfortable, I almost hate to wake him up to go home."

"You're done for the day, then?"

"Ja." The memory of her afternoon tipped her mouth up into a smile. "Thank you for watching Matthew for me. The tour for today was the biggest one so far. Kayla brought three vans, and they just about cleaned my shelves off."

"That's *gut!*" Jeremiah smiled down at her, and the genuine pleasure in his eyes warmed her heart.

There was a special sweetness in sharing happy news with someone who was just as glad about it as she was. She used to wait impatiently for Henry to come in from the fields in the evenings, so she could share some tidbit with him. She'd not realized how much she'd missed that...until now.

"You'll need more things brought up from the cellar, then," Jeremiah was saying. "You tell me what you want, and I'll take care of it."

As if he didn't have enough to do. But there was no doubt she'd need his help. She could bring up a lot of the items easily enough, but some would be too heavy.

"Denki. The tours are really helping the store. And so are those flyers. I don't think I've really thanked you for doing that."

"It was nothing."

"That's not so. Kayla said the store owners only put them up because everyone in Owl Hollow thinks so highly of you."

Jeremiah studied her, and a muscle twitched in his jaw. "Not everyone does."

"Well, I do," Anna assured him softly.

He hesitated, then he drew in a breath. "I don't... I don't talk much about what happened with Barbara—the girl I was going to marry. But, if you're willing to listen, I'd like you to know the whole of it."

She lifted her chin. "You can tell me or not, Jeremiah. Whatever you want."

"I think maybe you were right earlier. It's time you and I were honest with each other." He drew a long breath. "The truth is, Barbara never wanted to marry me. It was her *daed* who wanted that. He'd no sons, see, and I'd worked for Samuel since I was ten, odd-jobbing. His farm was next to ours, so it was easy, and my *mamm* was a widow, and not left well off. It was just me and her, and we needed the money and the extra vegetables and such he'd send over. We were thankful for that, so I made sure to be a good worker."

"I'm sure you were," she murmured.

"Barbara was his youngest, and the closest to my age. She was a sweet girl." He cleared his throat, looking embarrassed. "Her sisters had all left home by then, married with families and homes of their own. Her *daed* started making little jokes about how much Barbara liked me. Nudging me in her direction. I thought he was doing it because she wanted him to. She didn't."

"But she agreed to marry you anyway?"

"That wasn't so much her fault. She was sweet, like I said, and didn't have much spirit, and she wanted to please her *daed*. She knew he needed help on the farm, and the fellow she did like the look of, Jonah Miller, well." Jeremiah seemed to be considering his words carefully. "He wasn't so strong as me, and he wasn't used to farm work. His family made buggies, and he planned on doing that, too."

"She said she'd marry you, even though she had feelings for somebody else?" Anna made it clear with her tone that she'd little sympathy for such a girl.

"Jonah hadn't spoken. I suspect Samuel had been discouraging him some. And then, you know, we got engaged. Those things are supposed to be kept secret, but word always gets out."

"*Ja*, it does."

"So then Jonah couldn't speak. And just before the wedding, I found Barbara crying behind the barn. Because she was too afraid to tell her father that she just couldn't stand the thought of marrying me."

"Jeremiah—"

"It wasn't her fault," he cut in. "But Samuel... The dairy farm meant a lot to him, and he'd gotten pretty fond of me, too, I think. He had everything set up just how he wanted it, and the wedding fixings were all paid for. So, I told her I'd talk to her father myself, tell him I was the one breaking things off. Then everybody could blame me." He looked at her. "I've never told anybody the whole truth of it. I didn't lie," he added quickly. "I just never would explain, except to say it was my decision. And it was, because I sure wasn't about to force that poor girl to marry me."

"Oh, Jeremiah." Anna shook her head slowly. "Did you... Did you love her?"

He took a careful pause before he answered. "If I didn't, I should have. Barbara is a nice girl, and she never meant to cause me or her *daed* any trouble. Looking back now, I can't say if I was so much in love with her or if it was more the idea of belonging to the Esh family, of having Samuel as my father-in-law. I just don't know anymore. I see things... a little different now. But I can say I meant to love her and be kind to her. I meant to be a good husband."

"I'm sure you did." Without thinking, she reached out and grasped his arm. "And you would've been, Jeremiah. I have no doubt about that."

He didn't answer her. In fact, she wasn't entirely sure he was listening. He seemed distracted.

"Thank you for being honest with me, Jeremiah. I just wish Barbara had been honest, too. She waited far too long to make her feelings clear, and it wasn't right for you to bear the burden of her mistake."

Her heart ached at the injustice of that. Jeremiah was being generous, but it was foolish of any girl to come that close to a marriage if her heart wasn't in it.

"That part was all right," he said absently. "I've got a good set of shoulders for carrying burdens, and I was a lot more used to trouble than Barbara was. Anyway, it took a while, but things worked out for the best. Well, for Barbara and Jonah, anyhow. I'm not so sure about Samuel. Last I heard, he was paying two teenaged boys to do the chores I did, and he wasn't too happy with their work, either."

"It serves him right," Anna said fiercely.

"*Ach*, now," Jeremiah protested. "He was kind to me for a lot of years, and—"

He trailed off without finishing the sentence, and belatedly she realized why he kept looking down.

She was still holding onto his arm—so tightly that her knuckles were pale.

"Oh!" She released him, blushing. "You're right. I shouldn't be speaking so about people I don't know and something that's none of my business. I'm sorry. I just… I like you, and—" She broke off. She was making this worse. "I'm sorry," she repeated.

"I'm not." He spoke the words softly. "I'm not sorry that you like me, Anna, although I've been having an awful hard time believing you could. Or should."

He looked into her eyes then, one long look, and she felt the force of it all the way down to her toes.

Then he leaned down and kissed her.

Chapter Twelve

Jeremiah hadn't made a habit of kissing girls. He'd had to work too hard during his growing-up years, and he'd had little time for singings or other social activities. The truth was, he'd only kissed Barbara a handful of times, even after they'd settled on being married. She'd seemed shy about such things, and he'd never pushed it.

Looking back now, of course, he realized that shyness hadn't had much to do with it. After the wedding had been called off, he'd driven by the Esh farm one moonlit evening and seen Barbara kissing Jonah beside his buggy. He'd turned his eyes away quick, but going by the glimpse he'd gotten, Barbara wasn't near so shy as he'd thought.

Jeremiah hadn't kissed any girls since—until now. So likely he wasn't the man to ask about such things. But if anybody had asked him, he'd have to say that kissing Anna Speicher was the sweetest thing a fellow could think of. So sweet and so simple and so perfectly natural that he could have stayed right here in this barn, holding this woman in his arms, kissing her for the rest of his days.

That was how he felt, but there was still the matter of what she thought about it. So finally, reluctantly, he cut the kiss short and opened his eyes.

Anna's eyes fluttered open, too. As she looked up at him,

he scanned her face, searching for some clue about how she was feeling.

The only thing he could tell for certain sure was that he'd surprised her.

That made two of them.

"Anna," he started gruffly. "I—"

That was as far as he got.

"Mamm!" Matthew's sleepy voice chirped behind them. Jeremiah looked over his shoulder. The little boy was scrambling up from the straw, rubbing his eyes.

Jeremiah realized he was still holding Anna's hands in his. He dropped them and took a step back. Anna's stunned gaze lingered on him just a second longer before she turned to her son.

"You've had a nice nap." Her voice sounded a little shaky. She leaned over to brush away the straw clinging to Matthew's clothes and hair. "Are you hungry? Would you like a cookie and some milk?"

"*Ja.* Sunny, too?" The dog barked sharply, as if seconding the plea.

Anna nodded. "I suppose so."

"And Big Jer-miah?"

Anna tensed. She looked up, her eyes meeting Jeremiah's. Clearly she wasn't sure what to say. "Well—"

"No cookies for me," he said quickly. "I haven't the time. Rain's stopped, and I've work waiting."

"We'd best let you get to it, then! Come on, Matthew."

She didn't seem too sorry to be leaving his company. And that meant the kiss had been a big mistake.

The happy warmth blooming in Jeremiah's chest went cold, like a fire doused with water. He leaned over to snag his hat from the straw pile. As he settled it on his head, he tried to think of the right thing to say, something that would wash the tension out of the air. Something that would set things right.

He came up empty.

Matthew and Sunny ran out of the barn door into the now bright afternoon, where the sun glistened on raindrops everywhere. Anna stood in the doorway watching them go. She started to follow them, then stopped and looked over her shoulder at him.

"Jeremiah?" She spoke softly, her expression uncertain. "Maybe later you'll have time for cookies. And then we can talk."

Jeremiah's heart, which had settled like a cold lump in the pit of his stomach, bobbed up as quick as a cork dropped in a pail of water.

"*Ja*, sure! I'll have time later." He'd have it, or he'd make it. "And we'll talk."

"All right."

For a second he thought she was about to say something else. But in the end, she simply turned away and followed her son into the brightness of the yard. Jeremiah watched the two of them making their way through the damp grass—he'd see about cutting that soon—the little dog dancing around them happily.

He stood where he was, his heart thudding heavily in his chest. It wasn't every day that a fellow saw everything he'd ever wanted right in front of him, framed in a barn door. Maybe not within his reach. Not yet, not for certain.

But that soft look in Anna's eyes—the way she'd said his name just then—that gave him hope. And that was more than he'd ever expected, given what all she knew about him.

That part made no sense, and that worried him. Of course, Anna was a widow with a little boy to raise. Pretty and *schmaert* as she was, that was a hard situation for any woman to be in. Maybe that was why she hadn't yet slammed the door fully between them—for much the same reason as Barbara hadn't at first.

Because even though Jeremiah wasn't the man of any woman's dreams, he had a strong back. He wasn't the fellow they really wanted, but he was decent enough and pleasant enough to get by with.

That would be enough for the church, he knew. Marriages, especially second ones, were often based more on common sense than romance. And if he was being honest— really honest—the truth was, it'd be enough for him, too.

More than enough.

He couldn't expect Anna to care for him, not in the way he'd started caring for her. He'd take whatever she was willing to give and count himself blessed.

Nee, he didn't mind being settled for. But what he did mind was the idea of Anna settling. For the likes of him, a man whose biggest achievement in life would be buying a farm Anna already owned.

Such a man could probably never make her half so happy as she could make him. And Anna deserved to be happy.

But now, after that kiss, he was well past the point of just walking away. He didn't know what to do. And when a man didn't know what to do, there was only one thing a man could do.

Jeremiah reached up slowly and took the hat back off his head. He looked up at the dusty eaves of the barn.

"Well, Gott, I love her." He said it out loud in the barn. "I love her with all my heart, but You knew that already, I reckon. And I love that little boy, too, like he was my own. I can't believe that she'd ever consider a fellow like me. But—" He stopped and swallowed. "If she did, I'd do my best by them. For the rest of my life, as long as I'm breathing air, I'll take care of them, as best I can. But the best a man like me can do…well. I'm just not sure that's enough."

He drew in a deep, hard breath. "So, I'm asking You for a kindness. You let me know. I'm none too quick in my thinking. Never have been. Never will be. You'll have to make it plain to me, so there's no way I can misunderstand. Make it plain if I've got what it takes to give Anna and Matthew a happy life. I'll give them everything I have in me, Gott. I just need You to let me know if that's going to be enough."

He waited, but there was no answer except the quiet drip of rainwater off the roof. So finally, he put his hat back on his head, squared his shoulders and walked outside to finish the day's work.

The following morning, Anna stared out the kitchen window at the gathering storm clouds as she packed the lunch cooler. Matthew sat at the table finishing up his breakfast. Susie stood by the screen door, sipping the last of her coffee and frowning at the fitful breeze tossing the branches of her young apple tree.

"This weather," Susie said for the third time. She shook her head.

"*Ja*, we're in for some rain," Anna said, but she wasn't really thinking about the weather or about the food she was packing, or even about Matthew, who'd gotten up that morning with a case of the summer sniffles.

Ever since Jeremiah had surprised her with that kiss yesterday, she hadn't been able to think about anything but that. It was becoming a problem.

Whenever she remembered the gentle firmness of Jeremiah's mouth on hers, the strength of his arms gathering her close, her stomach went swirly, and her knees turned wobbly. Which, she kept reminding herself, was plenty silly.

She wasn't some sixteen-year-old *maidel*—going swimmy-headed over a simple kiss. She was a grown woman. She'd been married. She was a *mamm*, for pity's sake.

Which meant she shouldn't go around kissing men in a barn in the first place. But if she did, she certain sure shouldn't be feeling so addled about it.

It made no sense, but there was no denying it. It was as if all her *gut* sense had leaked out, replaced by fluttery feelings—and a smidge of guilt.

Henry had been a pleasant man, and a handsome one, and they'd had a happy marriage together in the little time they'd had. She'd loved him, and after his death, she'd felt sure she could never kiss a man again without thinking of him. It was one of many reasons the idea of marrying again hadn't felt right. It would be unfair, she'd thought, to the other fellow, having to stand in Henry's shadow.

Maybe Jeremiah was just too big a man to stand in anybody's shadow because when he'd kissed her—

"Anna?"

Susie's voice made Anna jump. "Oh! I'm sorry—did you say something?"

"I did." Her friend studied her, one eyebrow cocked. "I asked you a question. Did you mean to put that whole jar of mayonnaise into the cooler?"

"Oh! *Nee*." Flustered, Anna dug out the jar. "Sorry, I was...um...daydreaming."

She'd better be more careful. She didn't want Susie to guess what had happened. If Susie had any idea that Jeremiah had kissed her, she'd redouble her matchmaking efforts, and Anna didn't need this to get any more complicated. Not until she figured things out for herself. And Susie was like a bloodhound when it came to sniffing out anything romantic.

Usually. But today, she was distracted by the weather. Susie hated storms.

"I don't like the look of that sky," Susie was saying now. "Maybe you shouldn't go to the store today, Anna."

"I don't think the weather's going to be that bad." Anna was used to Susie's nervousness about storms. Her husband had been killed in a buggy accident while driving in a thunderstorm. Lightning had struck a tree on the side of the road, spooking his horse, who had crossed the lane into oncoming traffic.

So Anna understood why her usually steady friend became uneasy whenever thunder rumbled. But she didn't share her fear of bad weather.

"Besides," Anna went on, closing the lid to the cooler. "Kayla is bringing another tour group out today. I can't afford to miss that many sales."

"The weather'll be worse by the afternoon, they think. I heard it at the bakery yesterday, some people were talking. Thunderstorms, they said, and maybe hail, too." Susie shuddered.

"Hail?" Anna bit her lip as she bent to wipe strawberry jam off Matthew's face, remembering the lush green plants flourishing in Jeremiah's field. Hail was bad news for farmers. One ten-minute storm could damage a crop badly, if the hail was big enough.

But Susie had only heard that there *might* be hail. And, of course, there might not be.

"I'm sure it's nothing to worry about," she said hopefully.

"The tour is supposed to visit the bakery, too, but Kayla will likely cancel," Susie warned her. "Those ladies don't like to get out in bad weather. I wish you'd seen about getting a phone out there at the store, so I could let you know."

Lately when Susie wasn't dropping broad hints about what a fine husband Jeremiah would make, she was pestering Anna to talk to Charley Coblentz about getting permission to install a phone at the store. While phones weren't allowed in homes in their community, exceptions were made for businesses.

Anna had been so busy that she hadn't spoken to the bishop yet—and to be honest, she was a little *naerfich* about approaching Charley anyway. Her *mamm* had said people were talking about her and Jeremiah. What if Charley wanted to discuss that? So, she'd been putting the talk about the phone off.

"Well, I suppose I'll figure it out when they don't show up," Anna said cheerfully. "Come on, Matthew, we'd best get on our way."

Susie leaned forward to squint up at the darkening sky. "Kayla will call the bakery if the tour isn't coming, but there's no way for her to get in touch with you out at the farm. If we have a customer from out your way, I'll send a note letting you know about the tour, and I'll pass along any serious warnings about the weather, too. If it gets too bad, you might want to leave your horse and buggy at Jeremiah's and see if you can find someone to drive you home."

Anna nodded, although she wasn't so sure she could. The Englisch folks they hired as drivers were wonderful people, but sometimes last-minute requests couldn't be granted. She tried never to ask unless it was really an emergency. Susie understandably thought every thunderstorm was an emergency, but Anna knew better.

Soon she and Matthew were rattling along in the wind-buffeted buggy, headed to the farm. It wasn't really raining yet, only sprinkling, and judging by the strength of the wind,

Anna guessed that the storm would blow quickly through before it could do much damage.

She hoped so. She hated the thought of hail pummeling the vegetables Jeremiah had worked so hard to grow. He didn't seem too worried about it, but she knew he needed every penny he could make out of this late summer crop.

As Matthew chattered happily beside her, Anna debated whether to mention what Susie had told her. Maybe she shouldn't. After all, there was nothing any farmer could do about hail—or any type of weather trouble, for that matter.

Such things were in Gott's hands, so there was probably no point in worrying Jeremiah about it. Anyway, she was worried enough for both of them.

Anna sighed as she flicked the reins on Bessie's back. *Please, Gott,* she prayed as she drove. *Spare his crop. Let the weather pass the farm by. Please—*

She blinked. This prayer—and the feeling of dread in her middle—felt awfully familiar. How many times had she prayed such prayers in the short time she and Henry had farmed? Too many to count.

With a farm, there was always something to worry about. Hail and high winds, insects, some new disease killing livestock. Too much rain or not enough. She'd tried to trust Gott with those things, but it had been hard sometimes. Hard to trust, and hard to accept that sometimes Gott didn't work things out the way she'd have liked.

Hard to see Henry pushing himself harder and harder trying to make the farm produce enough to live on. Dealing with one trouble coming on top of another.

Everyone experienced hardship in life. Anna knew that, but it did seem like farmers got an extra share. And so did their families.

When she'd fallen in love with Henry, she'd been young

and full of hopeful dreams. The fact that he was a farmer hadn't given her a second's pause. She'd not grown up on a farm, so she hadn't known what to expect.

Now, she did. She glanced down at Matthew, swinging his short legs happily as they rolled down the road. Everyone said he looked more like her than his *daed*, and he did have her hair and her eyes. But every now and then he'd hold his mouth a certain way and look sideways at her the way Henry used to do. And in those brief seconds, he looked so much like his father that it made her breath catch in her throat.

But other times just lately, he would crouch down to gently touch a leaf, his eyes shining with wonder. Or she'd see him standing beside the store, his legs planted far apart, his chubby hands fisted on his hips, gazing over the fields with a big grin on his face.

Henry had liked the farm well enough, but in those moments it wasn't Henry Matthew reminded her of.

Memories flitted through her mind one after the other, as if she were turning the pages of a book. Jeremiah, coming in from the fields, streaked with dirt and sweat, tired lines etched deeply in his face. His eyes lighting up when he saw Matthew, no matter how worn out he was. How he steadily went about his work—and helped with hers, more often than she'd ever expected.

His face and arms mottled with welts after rescuing Matthew from the yellow jackets—and never complaining, nor even defending himself when she'd spoken to him so unfairly.

The way he'd held her when he'd kissed her, as if she was made of spun glass. As if it was safe for her to be fragile.

Because he wasn't.

And he would raise his sons—should he have any—to

be like him. He'd show them how to be strong. To be kind, and to be humble. To be a steady, quiet and faithful man. Because that was who Jeremiah was, himself, and he knew no other way.

For the same reason, he'd show them how to love the land. To smile over green growing things and to care for them, patiently and tirelessly. Since he made no excuses for himself, he'd also teach them to work themselves into the very ground they plowed if that's what it took to provide for their families.

Because Jeremiah Weaver was born to be a farmer. There was just no getting around that. Whether he bought this particular farm or not, that would never change.

Anna blinked back tears and snapped the reins on Bessie's back to speed her up. She didn't have much time before she'd have to open the store. She needed to get to the farm and break out the cookies in the lunch cooler and hope Matthew felt well enough to romp around the yard with Sunny for a few minutes.

It was time for her and Jeremiah to have that talk.

Chapter Thirteen

He'd been listening out all morning, waiting. The minute Jeremiah heard Anna's buggy turning into the yard, he stopped hilling the corn and started down the row toward the gate carrying his hoe, Sunny tagging behind. Although he walked at his usual pace, his heart pounded as if he were running.

He'd done a lot of thinking and praying since yesterday. He couldn't say Gott had given him any definite answer, but during a long and mostly sleepless night, he'd come to one decision, at least.

He wasn't sure of much, not yet. But he was sure of one thing. Kissing Anna yesterday had been the most honest thing he could have done. Probably not the smartest thing—in fact, it might've been downright foolish. Time would tell.

But given how he was feeling, whatever else it had been, that kiss had been honest—more honest, maybe, than his going around pretending he wasn't falling more for her with every day that passed. And now he needed to keep on being honest with her.

He'd surprised her yesterday, kissing her out of the blue like that. And they'd not had any chance to talk it over after. He knew what that kiss meant on his side of things. Now he needed to hear Anna's side of it. It wasn't a conversation he was looking forward to—partly because it would be a golden opportunity for her to tell him straight out what she probably ought to tell him—that there was no hope at all for the two of them.

That wasn't what he wanted to hear. But if it was the truth, the sooner he heard it, the better, and he'd take it as Gott's answer to his prayer—whether he liked it or not.

Anna wouldn't have much time before opening the store, but maybe he could get the words out quick. The words that ought to be said before a fellow kissed a woman, but better late than never, he guessed.

He hoped.

She'd climbed out of the buggy and was reaching up to help Matthew down. The barn and the white farmhouse were behind them, gleaming against a gray and sullen sky. Anna wore a rosy pink dress today and Matthew a light green shirt, and the picture they made, smiling at each other, nearly stopped Jeremiah's heart cold.

He swallowed hard and lengthened his strides. He didn't know—yet—if Anna and Matthew were Gott's will for his life. But one thing was for certain sure. If his own feelings were all that counted, he'd be talking to the bishop already.

As Anna swung Matthew down to the grass, she caught sight of Jeremiah. She straightened slowly, and her face turned as pink as her dress.

"Jeremiah," she said as soon as he came within earshot. "I was hoping to see you this morning. I wanted—"

"I sick," Matthew interrupted sadly.

"Sick?" Distracted, Jeremiah frowned down at the boy. Sure enough, the end of the child's nose was pink, and his eyes looked watery. "You're sick?" He looked up at Anna. "What kind of sick?"

"Just a summer cold," she said. "Nothing serious, but

he'd best stay inside with me today, out of the wet. Susie says the storm that's blowing in is likely to be a bad one."

"Likely." Jeremiah breathed a sigh of relief. The boy was all right, then. Summer colds were nothing serious.

He turned his attention back to Anna. She seemed uneasy, ruffling Matthew's hair over and over again with a restless hand. She glanced back toward the store.

"I have a tour coming today," she said. "Or at least, they're supposed to come. Susie says they often cancel if the weather's bad."

Susie. Jeremiah flinched as a new idea occurred to him. He hadn't thought about Susie. Likely Anna would have told her all about the kiss. Women talked about such things. He could well imagine what Susie would think, and he wondered what she'd said to Anna.

Plenty, he was sure, given Susie's fondness for matchmaking. He hoped she hadn't tried to push Anna into anything.

"You and I should probably talk," Anna was saying now.

Jeremiah glanced down. Matthew had knelt on the ground to fondle Sunny's ears and didn't seem to be paying attention. "I expect so, *ja.*"

Anna swallowed and lifted her chin. "I'm not sure… exactly what that meant…" The color in her cheeks grew rosier. "What happened yesterday."

There it was. He couldn't have gotten a better opening if he'd ordered one out of a catalog.

"What it meant yesterday is simple enough." He switched to English to keep Matthew from following the conversation. "I have feelings for you, Anna. I'd never have kissed you, otherwise. What it means now, today…what it could mean tomorrow… That's a lot harder to figure."

Anna's eyes remained fixed on his. He couldn't read her expression. "I don't understand," she said.

She was so pretty, standing there, her dress ruffled by the breeze, a strand or two of golden hair escaping from her *kapp* to twirl against her cheek. Jeremiah quickly dropped his eyes down to his boots.

If he didn't, he'd never say what needed saying.

He cleared his throat. "I told you about what happened before. With Barbara."

"You did. And it didn't sound to me like much of it was your fault."

He darted a look at her. She was still watching him, her bottom lip caught in her teeth, her blue eyes worried.

He looked back at his boots.

"Then I probably didn't explain it too well. More of it was my fault than wasn't. Once she'd agreed to marry me, Barbara was my responsibility to look after. I should have asked her more questions, made sure of what she was feeling. I didn't, because deep down I guess I didn't really want to hear the answer. Back then, I wanted the life that would have come with marrying Barbara. I wanted it an awful lot." He looked back up at her, determined to be honest. "I want this one, too, now. Even more. You. The boy." He looked around at the fields, a dull green now, the plants tossed by the wind. "A family of my own. This farm. But what I want isn't what matters most. The truth is, it's what matters the least. I can't stand the thought of ever making you unhappy."

She made a soft protesting sound. "Jeremiah—"

He knew better than to stop now, before he'd said the rest of it, so he went on. "I put the cart in front of the horse that time. I didn't ask Barbara the right questions, and I'm not proud to admit it, but I don't think I prayed about it once. I'm praying about this, now, so that part's all right. But I haven't asked you any questions, either. I haven't even asked if you…if you think that maybe you could ever…"

He couldn't believe he was saying this, and he sure wasn't doing a *gut* job of it. He cleared his throat again, roughly.

"Big Jer-miah sick, too," Matthew announced sadly.

Startled, Jeremiah looked into Anna's face, and they laughed at the same time.

"Nee," Anna said softly. "He's not sick."

Their eyes held, and something he saw in hers made his heart lift. "I don't know about that," he said. "I sure haven't been feeling like myself just lately." A car turned into the driveway. Anna's first customer had arrived.

It was now or never.

"I'll understand if you've no interest in me." He had to make himself say it. "You can tell me so. That's fine." It wasn't fine with him, but that wasn't Anna's problem. "Or, if you're not…sure…then you can say that you'll pray about this, same as I'm doing. For Gott to make this clear for both of us."

"Excuse me?" A woman had stepped out of the car. She waved at them. "Are you open?"

"Ja! I'm open!" Anna called. She turned back to Jeremiah. "I—"

"Miss? I'm in a bit of a hurry!" the woman called again. "Would you mind?"

"I'm coming! Jeremiah—"

"It's all right. You'd best go see to your work. I've said all I need to say," Jeremiah told her. He leaned over to give Matthew's hair a tousle. "You get to feeling better, little one. There'll be beans to pick before we know it."

He made it three steps toward the barn before Anna spoke sharply behind him.

"You know, just because you've said what you need to say doesn't mean I'm done talking."

She was right, of course. He'd known she wasn't done talking. He'd cut her off because he didn't really want to hear what he expected her to say.

He turned around slowly. "I'm sorry. Say your piece. I'm listening."

She swallowed. "You're a kind man, Jeremiah. A *gut* man. But I never really planned to get married again. And you're a farmer. And I just don't see—" She stopped and sighed.

He braced himself for the worst and waited, but Anna didn't finish the sentence.

"Miss!" the customer called again. She sounded irritated.

Anna glanced back, looking pretty irritated herself. But to his surprise, instead of heading in that direction, she walked toward him, leading Matthew by the hand. Tilting her head back, she looked up into his face.

"But," she said, "what I told you yesterday was true. I like you. In fact, I like you real well, Jeremiah. So I'll pray, too. And I guess we'll see."

Then she swung Matthew up into her arms and hurried back to where her customer was waiting.

Jeremiah stood where he was watching until she vanished into the store building. The wind was kicking up, and the first drops of rain splatted on his face, cold and hard.

Susie was right about this storm. It would be a bad one. He'd best finish hilling his corn before the wind laid it flat. He turned and started back toward the garden.

Even from here he could see that his plants were already being roughly tossed, and the storm was barely getting started. That wasn't *gut*. It was certain sure nothing for any farmer to smile about.

But Jeremiah was smiling. And his smile grew bigger with every step he took, as he played Anna's words over and over in his head.

The truth is, Jeremiah, I like you real well.

Of course, liking a man wasn't the same as loving him. He'd learned that lesson the hard way.

But it was enough for a fellow to hope on.

Two hours later, Anna stood behind the counter and listened to Martha Coblentz chatter—or she tried to listen. She was having a hard time paying attention.

Martha had stopped by with a message from Susie. Kayla had phoned the bakery, canceling the scheduled tours due to the worsening weather forecast. Since this was Martha's first visit to the Farmhouse Pantry, the bishop's wife had lingered to shop—and to talk.

"Poor Susie's having a hard day." Martha scooted a jar of Elizabeth's blueberry jam over for Anna to add to the total. "You know how much she hates bad weather."

"*Ja*, she does." Anna began adding up the prices on her pad.

She was thankful for the sale. This weather wasn't doing her business any favors. The impatient woman—who'd only bought a tiny jar of nutmeg after all that fussing—Martha and a nice Englisch lady who was still shopping had been her only customers all morning.

That was probably just as well, because Matthew needed more attention than usual. He wasn't feeling terribly sick—which was part of the problem. He wanted to go outside, and he didn't like staying in his play area behind the counter.

Of course, Matthew wasn't the only distraction. Anna's thoughts kept drifting to her talk with Jeremiah—to the way he'd looked when he'd said he had feelings for her. And how his face had lit up when she promised him she'd pray.

When she'd pulled Bessie to a stop beside the store this morning, she'd been convinced in her mind that there was no future for her with Jeremiah. But now her heart felt like that bit of old rope Matthew and Sunny liked to play tug-of-war with.

One minute she was reminding herself of the decisions she'd made after Henry's death, sensible decisions about the future she wanted for herself and Matthew—a future that definitely didn't involve this farm. Then she found herself spinning daydreams of a future with a tall, gentle man. One with kind brown eyes and a special way of smiling at her that almost made her forget—

"Anna? Have you figured up how much I owe you?"

Anna blinked at the half-done receipt, the pen idle in her hand. She started writing again. "Almost. Sorry."

"Oh, this nasty weather's got everybody distracted," Martha said with a smile.

After she and Martha settled up, Martha picked up her bag and smiled. "As *naerfich* as Susie was, she still badgered me to ask Charley about you getting a phone out here."

Anna laughed. "Susie can be *schtubbich* sometimes."

"She can. But that's not always a bad thing. Half the marriages in our county only happened because of that woman's stubbornness." The older woman tsked her tongue. "I sure felt sorry for her today, though. When someone said there was a chance of tornadoes, she dropped a whole tray of caramel rolls. Emma Smucker finally told her to just go home."

"Oh, no!" Anna frowned. The mention of tornadoes didn't bother her as much as the dropped caramel rolls. Susie was ashamed of her fear of storms, so she hid it as best she could. If she'd been shaky enough to get sent home, she must be very upset. "Maybe I should close up and go home myself. Susie might appreciate some company."

"If you're going, I'd leave before it starts raining again."

Martha craned her neck and peeked out the window. "I see Jeremiah heading up from the field. That garden is growing so well—I'll pray it doesn't get damaged in this storm. Now, I suppose I'd best take my advice and start home myself!"

Anna glanced at the Englisch lady, who was still shopping. The cloth bag looped over her shoulder was bulging, and she'd brought two large sacks of wheat berries over to the counter, too. Not a customer Anna wanted to rush out the door.

"Martha, before you leave, would you go speak to Jeremiah? Let him know that I'm planning to close the store early so I can be with Susie." She spoke in English, hoping the customer would take the hint and hurry up a little.

"I could." Martha studied Anna with a lifted eyebrow. "If you think he needs to know."

Anna hated the flush she felt coloring her cheeks. "Oh, Jeremiah and I keep a friendly eye out for each other. If I'm leaving early, he'll appreciate knowing. That's all."

Matthew had hopped up at the mention of Jeremiah's name. He tugged on Anna's dress. "Go see Big Jer-miah? Please?"

Martha's eyebrow went up another notch.

"They're friends, too," Anna explained uncomfortably.

"Well, isn't that nice?" The older woman's eyes twinkled with happy suspicion. She glanced out the window. "Those clouds are getting darker, and I'd like to get home before it gets rough again. Here." She flipped her receipt over and took Anna's pen, scribbling on its blank side. "We'd best write Jeremiah a note. Your boy can run it to him, can't he? He's gone into the barn, so it's not far, but my knee is troubling me and I'd just as soon not make the walk."

"Ja!" Matthew agreed happily.

A note? For Jeremiah? Anna bit her lip, but she couldn't

argue without explaining why writing a note to Jeremiah wasn't such a *gut* idea.

"I'm keeping Matthew inside today," she said quickly. "He has a cold."

"It's only a short walk." Martha had raised too many children to worry over a cold. "And he'll come straight back after he gives Jeremiah the note. Won't you, child?"

Matthew nodded, and Anna watched uneasily as Martha handed him the slip of paper. The bishop's wife shepherded the child to the door and pointed toward the barn. "There he is. Remember to come right back!"

After Matthew ran outside, the note clutched in his hand, Martha returned to the counter and picked up her bag.

"I hope you can close up soon and get home yourself." She cut a sharp look at the last customer, who was still browsing, apparently immune to hints. "It's kind of you to go see about Susie. You're a *gut* friend."

"She's been a *gut* friend to me," Anna said.

Martha chuckled. "Maybe an even better one than you know. The phone isn't the only thing she's pestered Charley about. He wasn't so sure this was a *gut* idea, you having your store here because it would mean two unmarried folks spending so much time alone. But Susie just about talked his ear off in the bakery, reminding him of your character and praising Jeremiah's. She said she felt certain sure this arrangement would lead to..." Martha paused as if choosing her words carefully. "A special friendship. And it looks like she was right. But then, she usually is."

With that—and a wink—Martha walked out into the wind-tossed yard and headed for her buggy.

Chapter Fourteen

Jeremiah squinted up at the sky and sighed. Bottom-heavy, dark gray clouds scudded across the sky, and the wind was getting fiercer. He didn't like the look of this storm.

Neither did Sunny. She'd been acting *naerfich* all day, so when her wagging tail thumped against his leg, he was surprised.

Until he looked out and saw Matthew running across the yard, grinning from ear to ear.

"Big Jer-miah!" The boy held out a fluttering paper. "Here."

"For me?" Confused, Jeremiah took the paper. *"Denki."*

The squeak and crunch of buggy wheels drew his eye to the Coblentz buggy, rolling out of the yard. Martha waved at him, and he waved back.

Martha must have sent him the note. Anna wouldn't have, understanding how long it would take him to puzzle it out.

Unless maybe it was something she didn't like to say to his face. He sent a cautious look at Matthew, but the boy was paying him no attention. He was tussling with Sunny on the ground, chortling as the dog licked his face. Jeremiah unfolded the note.

Not Anna's handwriting, he noted with relief. He knew

what that looked like from the chalkboard. So, this was from the bishop's wife, then. But why would Martha Co-blentz be writing him a note?

He chewed on the inside of his cheek as he worked out the words. *S-u-s-i-e*. Susie. *Susie is...u-p-s-e-t*.

"I go," Matthew announced sadly. "Mamm said. Bye, Sunny! Bye, Big Jer-miah!"

That's right. Anna hadn't wanted the little fellow out in the wet. And everything was plenty wet already. The rain had been coming in short bursts all morning, and from the look of those clouds, more was on the way.

"Go on, then. Sunny can see you to the door."

Matthew beamed. "*Kumm*, Sunny!"

The little boy scampered back across the damp grass, the little dog running at his heels. Matthew rounded the front of the store, out of Jeremiah's sight.

Sunny didn't immediately reappear. She was probably hanging around the doorway, hoping for a cookie. She'd get one, too, if Matthew had anything to say about it.

He hoped they'd save a few for him. Of course, it wasn't really the cookies he was looking forward to. He was anxious to talk more with Anna, so he could watch her smile, hear her laugh. The snacks Susie sent might be sweet, but they'd never be so sweet as that.

Susie. Jeremiah looked back down at the note in his hand. Several lines of writing flowed after the words he'd managed to read, written in a hurried script.

So, Susie was upset, and since he was the one standing here holding the note, it must have something to do with him.

He wasn't sure what was going on, but most likely the note had something to do with Anna. Could be Susie didn't like how slow things were moving after that kiss. Likely the kindhearted meddler thought they should be talking to the bishop already—which might be how Martha had gotten involved.

He frowned. He hoped Susie hadn't gone that far. Jeremiah would've liked things to be moving quicker himself, but Gott answered prayers in His own time. And this?

He had to be sure about this, for Anna's sake.

A gust of wind hit the barn, and Jeremiah winced. He'd noticed earlier that a sheet of tin on the barn roof had come loose, and now he heard it flapping. If he didn't nail that down, it was likely to go flying off. He'd better tend to it before the weather got worse.

He folded up the note and stuck it in his pocket. He had no time to finish reading it now, and this wasn't something he could ask Anna's help with. He wouldn't know for sure until he'd read it for himself, but if Susie and Martha Coblentz really were trying to push things along, he didn't want Anna to know.

No woman was ever going to be pushed into marrying him, not by her father and not by a matchmaker or a bishop, either. Until he heard from Gott and from Anna herself, there was nothing for him to do but wait. It was as simple as that.

He walked into the barn to find the nails and the hammer he'd need to secure the sheet of tin. Not too easy a job, climbing up on the roof to nail it down in this weather, but he'd just have to do the best he could. It would've been wiser to have done it earlier, when he'd first noticed the trouble. And normally he would've. But lately he'd been a little...distracted.

He heard the rumble of an Englischer's car starting up. Anna's last customer must be leaving. He pulled out half a dozen nails and stuck them between his lips for easy carrying. He'd need his hands free to climb the ladder.

Anna should take Matthew and go home herself. Maybe he'd walk up to the store and tell her so. Or better yet, she could take shelter in the farmhouse until the worst of this blew over. He trusted the farmhouse's sturdy walls and roof more than the store building.

Another gust of wind hit, making loose tin on the roof shriek. Jeremiah picked up a hammer and sighed, thinking about his plants out in the field. This wind would be no friend to them, particularly not to the corn. He'd hilled it as best he could, but—

The wind grew stronger, shuddering the barn walls. Then Sunny started barking.

And she didn't stop.

Jeremiah paused, listening. He'd never heard the dog bark like that except once—when the yellow jackets had gotten after Matthew. Something was wrong. He set down the hammer and walked to the door.

Sunny stood midway between the barn and Anna's store, facing the east. Her stubby legs were braced against the heavy wind, which blew her ears and fur back flat. She kept barking frantically, like she was trying to scare something away.

Jeremiah looked to his left, and his heart floundered. The clouds were low and dark, with an ugly greenish tinge—and they were starting to whirl.

He spat the nails onto the ground and took off at a run. The furious wind fought him every step of the way. Branches and twigs whipped past him, gravel and dirt stinging his cheeks. He burst into the store, panting.

Anna was behind the counter gathering her belongings. Matthew stood beside her. They froze and stared at him, eyes wide.

"We need to get to the cellar, Anna. Now."

Her face drained of color, but when she spoke her voice was carefully calm. "All right. Come along, Matthew. We're going up to the house for a while."

Matthew smiled. "Sunny, too?"

"Sunny, too," Jeremiah assured him. He looked at Anna. "Hurry."

She picked Matthew up and hurried across the room. Together they walked out into the strength of the rising storm.

The wind was hard for him to manage against, but it was almost impossible for Anna. She staggered, blown sideways by its force. He pulled Matthew out of her arms. "I'll carry him!" he shouted.

He wasn't sure if she heard him. The words were blown away as fast as he spoke them. But she nodded, so she understood.

He shifted Matthew to his left arm and put his right one around Anna, using his strength to keep her steady. Together they struggled across the yard, heading for the cellar door.

He'd never measured this distance, nor paid any attention to it. It had never seemed much to think about. But now he wished he knew exactly how far it was. Every step was a battle, and the branches hurtling from the trees were thicker. Sunny was trying to keep up with them, and she yelped sharply as a branch winged her. Anna stopped and leaned over, gathering the little dog into her arms.

Jeremiah glanced over Anna's head toward the east. No funnel, not yet, but the swirling was worse. It looked as if the sky was boiling, and hail had begun to pelt them. It was the size of marbles, and it hit with force.

Anna stopped again and nodded toward the cellar. "Go!" She looked pointedly down at Matthew in his arms, then back up at Jeremiah. "Faster," she mouthed. Her eyes pleaded with him.

His heart went cold. She was telling him to leave her, to take Matthew to the cellar. He shook his head.

"We can make it."

She looked back toward the gathering storm. Then she reached over with her free hand and clutched his arm tight, her eyes begging him.

"Please." He read the word on her lips. The she pushed him as hard as she could—which wasn't very hard at all. "Please."

He could see terrified tears in her eyes. For a few horrible seconds, he balanced his whole world, everything he wanted, against them, against what she was asking him to do.

Then he moved.

He ran for the cellar, ducking under the hurtling branches. He set Matthew down on the ground, sheltering the boy from the hammering hail as best he could while he fought open the doors. Then he carried the child down the stairs and set him on the floor.

"You stay there. Stay right there!" Jeremiah ordered sternly. Matthew nodded, his eyes—eyes like Anna's—huge with fear.

Jeremiah took the steps three at a time. The minute he stepped outside, the wind hit him like a charging bull. Somewhere, dimly, he heard the sharp tinkle of broken glass.

Anna was slowly fighting her way across the yard, her head down, her skirt whipping around her, still clutching Sunny against her body. A branch as thick as his arm flew over her head, nearly stopping his heart. He ran toward her, and she looked up at him.

She didn't try to speak, but he knew from her reproach-ful expression what she was thinking—she wasn't happy he'd left Matthew alone.

He didn't care. And anyway, the boy wouldn't be alone for long. He swung Anna up into his arms, dog and all, and sprinted for the cellar.

The minute her feet hit the steps, Anna hurried down to where Matthew huddled on the floor, quietly crying. She set a shaking Sunny down, then knelt, gathering her son into her arms.

Jeremiah closed the doors, plunging the cellar into dark-ness. He sank down on the steps, his heart racing, his knees like jelly. A second later, he heard a soft hiss, and a light glowed. Anna had lit one of the kerosene lamps.

"Are you all right? Both of you?" he demanded roughly.

She looked up at him, her light flickering over her face. Setting the lamp down carefully on a small wooden shelf, she walked toward him. Matthew shuffled behind, sniffling, clutching a handful of her dress. She stopped at the base of the steps and reached up to touch his wet and dirty boot.

"We're all right, Jeremiah," she said quietly. "Every-thing's all right now. Thanks to you."

Then, finally, he could breathe.

Anna had never seen a man so shaken. Jeremiah had dropped onto the steps as if his legs wouldn't hold him up, and he hadn't moved. His dark hair was tousled and wild, and some bit of flying debris had scored a scratch across one cheek.

He didn't answer her. He sat still for so long, not speak-ing, that she grew concerned.

"Jeremiah? Are *you* all right?"

He looked up at her, as if coming out of a daze. He pushed up to his feet. She backed away as he came heavily down the steps.

"You're really all right? You and the little one?" he asked again.

"*Ja*, we're fine. We're both fine," she assured him.

"Then I'm all right, too," he said.

Then, to her astonishment, his arms went around her, and he pulled her close. So close that she could feel the thud of his heart through his rain-soaked shirt.

The only other time she'd been in Jeremiah Weaver's arms like this, he'd held her lightly, gently. Now he held her so tightly she could barely breathe, and she could hear him whispering into her hair. He spoke so softly, though, that she couldn't make out what he was saying.

He was praying, she realized. And she should be, too. She closed her eyes, but she was so rattled that no words would come except *Thank You, Gott. Thank You.* Over and over again.

Finally he released her. He studied her, his eyes moving over her face, as if reassuring himself. Then he breathed a long, slow breath, leaned over and picked Matthew up. The boy nestled his head against Jeremiah's broad shoulder.

"Bad storm, Big Jer-miah," the boy snuffled.

"Just a lot of wind and rain," Jeremiah said. "We're safe down here. Gott's looking out after us. It'll be over soon."

"I all wet," Matthew announced sadly.

"We all are," Anna said. As if on cue, Sunny shook herself, flapping water everywhere. That surprised a giggle out of Matthew.

"Well, we're even wetter now," Jeremiah said with a chuckle.

Anna smiled, thankful he was acting more like himself.

They stood together, listening to the frightening sounds coming from above them until finally the noises grew quieter.

"I think it's over," she whispered.

"Wait here." Jeremiah went up the steps and pushed open the doors.

Gray light flooded into the cellar, along with droplets of leftover rain. Jeremiah walked up a few more steps and looked around.

"*Ja*, the storm's spent," he said. "Come on up."

He stepped outside and waited at the cellar opening as Anna led Matthew up the stairs. She looked out at the yard, littered with leaves and limbs and melting hail. Damage was everywhere. A few trees along the edge of the yard were down, and part of the barn's roof was missing. The store building seemed mostly intact, although the back window was broken. No doubt the rain had ruined some things inside, but it didn't look too bad.

The wind had died down to a fitful breeze, and patches of blue showed through the ragged clouds. It was as if the day had flung a tantrum, and now it was over.

Anna scanned the disheveled farm. "Was it a tornado?"

"Maybe. It didn't hit us head-on if it was. We can be thankful for that."

"*Ja*," Anna agreed. "The weather looked nasty all morning, but it got bad so fast!" She shook her head. "Susie's going to fuss even more about me getting a phone out here. That way she can let me know when the weather gets bad like this."

Jeremiah had been looking around the farm, too, but he turned his head so fast that it startled her. "Susie wanted to warn you about the weather?"

"*Ja*, Susie's *naerfich* about storms, she pays close attention to weather forecasts. But a storm like this comes up so quick there's just no time, unless you have a phone to use."

He looked away again, over the fields. His color had come back nearly to normal, but now it washed out of his cheeks again. She realized what he was looking at.

The vegetable garden.

"Oh, Jeremiah." She walked across the yard, stepping around the downed branches to get a better look. She couldn't tell much at this distance, but what she could see didn't look promising. This morning the garden had been green and lush. Now, it was nearly laid flat.

Anna shook her head sadly, remembering all the hours of hard work Jeremiah had put into that field. It was too bad, it really was.

But, like it or not, this was farming.

She looked over her shoulder. She'd half expected Jeremiah to follow her, but he stood where she'd left him in the yard, studying a scrap of paper in his hand. He'd set Matthew down, and the little boy was chasing Sunny happily around the messy yard, the terror of the storm already forgotten.

As she walked back across the yard, she tried to think of something to say, something encouraging. She wasn't able to come up with much.

"Well." She put her hand on his arm. "It could have been worse."

"It was my fault." He looked at her, his eyes stricken.

"Vass?" Anna frowned. "Of course it wasn't your fault. It was a storm. It was nobody's fault."

He silently held out the paper. It took Anna a second to recognize the note Martha had scribbled on the back of her receipt—ages ago, it seemed.

She glanced down at it, then up at him. "I don't understand."

"Susie did warn us about the storm. She sent me a note, by Martha Coblentz. I can't… I haven't had time to figure it all out, but I know it says she's upset about storms. I got that much. She sent word, and I didn't read enough of it to understand that she was letting me know so I could look after you."

"*Nee*, Jeremiah," Anna said quickly. "You don't understand—"

"I understand enough." Jeremiah had one of the strongest faces she'd ever seen. Sometimes, when he was straining to lift something heavy or to drive a post into the ground, his jaw looked as if it was made of stone. But now it looked more like it was made of chalk.

He looked out over the wind-pummeled field. "I understand that Gott has said no. I asked Him to show me if I could…if a man like me could take care of you, Anna. If I could make you and Matthew happy, keep you safe."

Her heart twisted. "Jeremiah—"

He shook his head. "I asked Him to make it plain. Seems like He did." He gestured around them. "Crop's gone, and it's too late to put in another one this summer. And that's the least of it. If I'd known that weather was coming, I'd have had you and Matthew safe in that cellar before it got so bad. But I didn't know because I couldn't read Susie's note fast enough. Looks to me like Gott's made His point good and plain, just like I asked Him to."

"But that note—" Anna started, but Jeremiah cut her off.

"I'm sorry, Anna. For kissing you and for…hoping for things I'd no right to hope for. And don't worry. I'll fix up this damage so you can sell the farm if that's what you want to do. But—and I know I've no right to give you any advice—think hard before you do. You may not have any love left for this farm, but that little one—" He nodded at Matthew. "He does. I know you want to make a store-keeper out of him, and maybe you can. But it looks to me like Gott's given him a heart for something else." He sighed and managed a sad chuckle. "And I can tell you, when the Lord makes a fellow a certain way, he might as well stick with the path laid out in front of him. Saves a lot of trouble in the long run, for him and everybody else."

Anna let a few long seconds stretch out. Then she put her hands on her hips and faced him down.

"Fine. You've got all that off your chest. Now are you done talking?"

Jeremiah had been looking over his flattened crops, but the sharpness in Anna's voice got his attention. He glanced at her, startled.

Her hair was mussed, her *kapp* was too far back on her head and her eyes were spitting blue sparks. This was a side of Anna he'd not seen before, and he wasn't quite sure how to answer.

So, he just told the truth.

"I've said all I need to say, I guess."

"Gut," she said irritably. "Now maybe you can listen. But first." To his astonishment, she tiptoed, put her hands on his cheeks and drew his face toward hers.

And she kissed him.

Not in a barn. Not in a shadowed buggy on a moonlit night. But right in the middle of the yard, as if she didn't care one bit who saw them.

He had no idea how long the kiss lasted. His brain had stopped working the minute her lips touched his.

Not long enough. That much he knew.

She pulled back a little, but she kept her hands where

they were, bracketing his face, and she stared fiercely up into his eyes.

"Now you listen to me, Jeremiah Weaver. First of all, that note wasn't a warning at all. It only said that Susie had gotten upset at work, and I was going home early to keep her company."

Jeremiah frowned as he thought that over. "I don't see how that changes much, Anna. Even if it had been a warning, I couldn't have read it in time to protect you. Gott still made his point there."

"You protected us just fine without any warning. I can read, Jeremiah, but I don't know that I could've carried Matthew to that cellar by myself, not in that wind. And I couldn't have run him halfway across a field to save him from yellow jackets, either." She glanced at her son, who, his cold forgotten, was happily chasing Sunny around the old oak tree. Gentleness replaced the fierceness in her face. "Maybe Gott's making a different point. Maybe all along He's been showing us how much we need each other, you and I."

He looked into her eyes—blue as the best summer sky—and some of the heaviness in his heart lifted.

But only some.

"I need you," he admitted gruffly. "Not so sure how far it runs the other way."

"Did you not hear anything I just said? I need you plenty, Jeremiah Weaver, and don't you ever forget it."

He wanted to believe that. He did. But… "You need a man who can do more than carry heavy things, Anna." He nodded toward the ruined field. "I was banking on those crops. Without them…" He trailed off.

"Without them, what? You can't buy the farm? We already own the farm, Jeremiah. And anyway, I have an idea. Pumpkins."

"Pumpkins." He was having a hard time following what she was saying.

We, she'd said. *We own the farm.* As if they were already a family.

Hope—wild and unlooked for—rose up and thundered in his ears, louder than the storm.

"That's right. We can plant fall crops. Pumpkins, cabbages, broccoli. Things like that. I'll sell them at the store, and I'm sure other stores will want them, too." She sighed and shrugged. "Hopefully, the next crop will do well. But if it doesn't, we'll think of something else. That's the way farming goes, Jeremiah. And now we'll have income from the store to help out whenever crops don't do as well, so that's a blessing."

She gave his cheek a gentle pat before finally taking her hands away. He caught them midway and held them tight.

"You said you didn't want to marry a farmer again, Anna. And make no mistake about it. That's what I'm asking for. I want to marry you."

"I know that." She twinkled a smile up at him. "Do you think I'd go kissing a fellow right here in my yard if I didn't think we'd be married before the year's out?"

"Before the year's out?" Jeremiah suddenly found it hard to breathe.

"Well, that seems sensible, ain't so? We've a lot of work to do, and it seems smarter to be settled in by winter. What do you think?"

"I think I love you, Anna." There was a lot he wanted to say, but at the moment, that was all he could get out. "*Nee*, I don't think. I know. With everything that's in me, I love you. You and Matthew, both."

Her eyes softened, and she gave his hands a squeeze. "I love you, too, Jeremiah." She huffed out a little sigh. "And *nee*, I never wanted to marry another farmer. But I do want to marry you." She smiled at him. "With everything that's in me."

"If I could be anything else, anything that would make you happier, I'd do it. And if you want me to, I'll try."

She was shaking her head before he finished. "I don't. Not anymore. You're not the only one Gott teaches lessons to. That storm was a reminder that I can't shut danger out of Matthew's life—or yours. I have to trust Gott's plan for all of us, even when I don't understand it. Especially when I don't understand it. When hard times come, I have to trust what I know about Gott—that He's *gut*, that He's faithful. Like I trusted you to get Matthew to the cellar. The minute you left me and started running across the yard with him, I knew he'd be all right."

Not much could've dimmed the joy Jeremiah was feeling. He'd never imagined he'd hear Anna saying such things to him, never thought such a future could belong to a man like him.

But the memory of that awful moment when he'd left Anna standing alone in the teeth of that storm… That returned him to earth with a thump. Until he'd made it back across the yard to her, until he'd had her safe down in that cellar…

He didn't think his heart had beat once.

"Anna, there's something I need to say to you. I'm not planning on being a hard-hearted husband." He gently smoothed her loosened hair back from her face. "Being strong is the only thing I've ever been much good at, but when it comes to you…" He shook his head. "I expect you can ask me for pretty much anything, and if there's any way I can give it to you, you'll have it. But there's one thing, Anna. Only one, that I never want you to ask. Because I'm telling you now, it'll kill me if you do."

Her eyes were fixed on his, a worry line puckering her brow. "What is it?"

"Never ask me to leave you behind again."

Relief and love washed over her face, and her low laugh mingled with the happy giggles and barks coming from the oak tree.

"You better not, Jeremiah Weaver," she whispered, tip-toeing up again, the promise of another kiss in her eyes. "You better not."

* * * * *

Dear Reader,

Welcome back to the small Amish community of Hickory Springs, Tennessee! Come on in, take a seat at a well-scrubbed kitchen table, and we'll settle in for a visit. Here, away from the hustle and bustle of the modern world, there's always time for a cup of tea and a friendly chat—and there's usually something delicious baking in the oven, too!

We have plenty to talk about! In this sweet little town, romance is blooming everywhere—in buggies and barns, on front porches and farms. Susie Raber—a local matchmaker specializing in hard-to-match couples—has certainly been staying busy! Now she's got her eye on widow Anna Speicher and gentle-giant farmer Jeremiah Weaver, and from the look of things, she's got her work cut out for her with these two!

I hope you enjoy this second trip to Hickory Springs as much as I did, my friend. I'm already looking forward to many more visits—and lots more happily-ever-afters! In the meantime, I'd love to stay in touch! Head over to laurelblountbooks.com and sign up to be a part of my favorite bunch of folks—my beloved newsletter subscribers! Every month I share photos, book news and gotta-try-it recipes. And, of course, you can always write to me at laurelblountwrites@gmail.com! I look forward to hearing from you!

Much love,
Laurel